Jessi and the Bad Baby-sitter

**Other books by
Ann M. Martin**

Rachel Parker, Kindergarten Show-off

Eleven Kids, One Summer

Ma and Pa Dracula

Yours Turly, Shirley

Ten Kids, No Pets

Slam Book

Just a Summer Romance

Missing Since Monday

With You and Without You

Me and Katie (the Pest)

Stage Fright

Inside Out

Bummer Summer

BABY-SITTERS LITTLE SISTER series
THE BABY-SITTERS CLUB mysteries
THE BABY-SITTERS CLUB series
(see back of the book for a more complete listing)

Jessi and the Bad Baby-sitter
Ann M. Martin

AN
APPLE
PAPERBACK

SCHOLASTIC INC.
New York Toronto London Auckland Sydney

Cover art by Hodges Soileau

No part of this publication may be reproduced in whole or in part, or stored in a retrieval system, or transmitted in any form or by any means, electronic, mechanical, photocopying, recording, or otherwise, without written permission of the publisher. For information regarding permission, write to Scholastic Inc., 730 Broadway, New York, NY 10003.

ISBN 0-590-47006-X

12 11 10 9 8 7 6 5 4 3 2 1   3 4 5 6 7 8/9

Printed in the U.S.A.   40

First Scholastic printing, October 1993

The author gratefully acknowledges
Suzanne Weyn
for her help in
preparing this manuscript.

Special thanks to
Beth Perkins
for her creative input, too.

CHAPTER 1

"Squirt, no!" I cried as I raced into the living room. My two-year-old brother was about to totter off the end of the coffee table.

He stood wide-eyed, flapping his arms wildly for balance. With a bound, I sprang across the room and caught him before he hit the floor.

Whew!

"Is he all right, Jessi?" asked my eight-year-old sister, Becca, rushing in from the kitchen.

I soothed Squirt, who was now squirming in my arms. "He's just scared. I forgot that he's climbing on everything lately. I can't take my eyes off him for a second."

Squirt's *Pokey Puppy* video was still playing on the TV. Not long ago, he would have sat quietly on his big down pillow and watched it peacefully. But in the last few weeks he'd turned into a little mountain goat, scrambling up everything he could find.

"He's okay. Let's finish the game," said Becca as Squirt's sobs faded. "I was just about to buy Boardwalk."

"Bring the Monopoly game in here," I suggested. "That way we can keep an eye on Squirt while we play."

Becca sighed loudly. "Do we have to? I'll have to move all that money and the cards and everything. The houses will slide around. Why can't he come into the kitchen while we play?"

"Because then he'll pull the pots out of the cupboard and we'll have to listen to him bang them," I explained. Squirt *loves* to bang, and it's hard on the ears if you're trying to do something else.

"Oh, all right," Becca grumbled.

Squirt looked at me, his long black lashes wet with tears. "Me boom," he pouted.

I smiled at him and nodded, stroking his soft hair. Baby-sitting for a toddler and an eight-year-old at the same time wasn't easy. There wasn't much you could do that would entertain both of them. I had to give Aunt Cecelia credit. She was out for a few hours today, but she usually takes care of them while my parents are out.

Aunt Cecelia came to live with us when Mama went back to work. What a difficult time that was! At first I couldn't get used to Aunt

Cecelia. I thought she was too strict and old-fashioned.

Adjusting to Aunt Cecelia was especially hard because I was still trying to adjust to living in Stoneybrook. That wasn't easy at first.

Some of our neighbors weren't thrilled when a black family moved in. This shocked and upset me. Our old neighborhood had been integrated, and color just wasn't a big deal. When we came to Stoneybrook it was the first time I'd ever felt different in any way.

But we stuck it out and things are much better. Our neighbors know who we are as people now. If any of them are still bothered, they keep it to themselves. And I've made some super terrific friends. (Whom you'll hear about very shortly.)

Not only that, I've also come to love Aunt Cecelia. I also appreciate how much she does for the family. And I'm sure glad I don't have to baby-sit for Squirt and Becca every afternoon after school.

Not that I don't like to baby-sit. In fact, I *love* to baby-sit. I even belong to a club called the Baby-sitters Club, which I'll tell you about later. But maybe I have a little less patience with my own brother and sister. Or perhaps I was just feeling overwhelmed with everything I had to do that week. My schedule suddenly seemed to have hit complete overload.

As it is, my schedule is plenty tight. I have school, ballet lessons twice a week, BSC meetings three times a week (BSC is short for Baby-sitters Club), and baby-sitting jobs all week long. (Since my best friend Mallory Pike and I are eleven, we only sit in the afternoons — or sometimes in the evenings for our own brothers and sisters. We're junior BSC members.)

All of this kept me busy enough, but then Dawn (one of the members) left just recently. Since then I've had to take more baby-sitting jobs than ever before. In fact, all the members have had to do that, and it's been hard on everyone.

Dawn was, and still is, a member of the BSC. The problem is that right now she's in California. She's living with her father and brother for the next six months. You see, Dawn is originally from California, but she and her brother came here with their mom when their parents divorced. Her brother then went back to California to live with their dad, so now Dawn's original family is split between two coasts. Dawn's mom remarried (she married her old high school sweetheart who happens to be the father of Mary Anne, another BSC member, but that's another story which I'll fill you in on later). Anyway, Dawn started miss-

4

ing her dad and her brother, Jeff, and California in general, so she went back to live with them for awhile.

Now we were one member short and swamped with work. Help!

"There, the board is all set up again," Becca announced as she lined up the land cards. "We can play now."

"Becca, what happened to all my houses?" I asked.

"They got caught in an earthquake," she said, biting her lower lip. "Actually, it was more like a tidal wave. I spilled the can of punch on the board when I was trying to move it. I told you it wasn't a good idea to move the board."

At least that explained why the board had suddenly taken on a pinkish tint. "Squirt, stop that," I said as Squirt began throwing the Monopoly money in the air. He just laughed and chewed on the property cards.

"It's no good!" Becca sighed, flopping over onto her back.

Just then, the phone rang. "Make sure he doesn't put any of the houses or hotels into his mouth," I told Becca as I stood up to answer the phone in the kitchen.

It was Wendy Loesser, a friend of mine from school. (I'm in sixth grade at Stoneybrook Middle School. So is Mallory, and so is Wendy.)

"How's it going?" Wendy asked.

"A little crazy. I'm baby-sitting right now." As I spoke, with the phone cradled between my shoulder and cheek, I knelt on the kitchen floor with a roll of paper towels, sopping up the punch that Becca had missed when she cleaned up.

"I just called to say hi. Nothing important," she said. "Want me to call you back later?"

I got to my feet and peeked into the living room. Squirt was ripping Monopoly money, which Becca was trying to wrestle away from him. "This isn't a good time for me to talk on the phone," I said. "But would you like to come over?"

"Sure," said Wendy. "I don't know where you live, though."

Wendy and I were sort of new friends. Lately we'd started walking to some of our classes together.

"I know where that is," said Wendy after I gave her my address. "I'll be there in about twenty — "

"Jessi!" Becca shrieked. "Come quick."

"Gotta go. 'Bye," I said, quickly hanging up. I darted into the living room. Becca was on her feet, pointing at Squirt. "He's got one, Jessi!" she cried. "I was watching him. I was! I don't know how he got it into his mouth, but he did."

6

"What? What's in his mouth?" I asked, trying to stay calm.

"I don't know. Something," said Becca.

Cautiously, I approached Squirt who sat with a mischievous gleam in his eye and his lips clamped shut. "Open up, Squirt," I said gently. I didn't want to excite him and have him swallow whatever was in his mouth. "Come on, open your mouth."

Squirt shook his head. He thought this was a funny game, but I knew that whatever was in his mouth could get stuck in his throat and choke him.

"Squirt, please!" I pleaded.

He shook his head again. Begging wasn't going to work. I needed a strategy. "Look, Squirt! Look what Pokey Puppy is doing," I said, pointing to the TV. Squirt looked, and his lips parted as he was distracted by the TV. Like lightning, my fingers were in his mouth fishing out the small silver Monopoly marker shaped like a boot. Squirt realized he'd been tricked and began to howl.

"Thank goodness." Becca sighed with relief.

What an afternoon it was turning out to be! I put away the Monopoly game and prayed Wendy would arrive soon. I was looking forward to some help and company.

As she'd been about to promise — before I so rudely hung up on her — Wendy rang the bell in about twenty minutes. By then, Becca and Squirt were watching a *Flipper* rerun on the cable channel.

When I opened the door, she was standing beside her bike, her short brown hair ruffled by the autumn wind. "Where should I put this?" she asked, nodding toward her bike.

"Around back," I said. "Then just come on in."

"Cut it out, Squirt," I heard Becca say as I returned to the living room.

He was on his feet, slapping the TV screen, yelling, "Flippy! Flippy!"

"Come on, I want to see this," Becca complained as she dragged Squirt away, which caused him to start crying all over again.

"Sounds pretty noisy in here," Wendy said, laughing, as she let herself in the front door.

Becca and Squirt stopped to stare at her. I think Wendy has a really pretty face. She has delicate features, big brown eyes, and a quick smile. "Hi, I'm Wendy," she introduced herself to the kids.

Becca gently set Squirt onto the carpet. "I'm Becca, which is short for Rebecca. This is pain-in-the-neck, Squirt. His real name is John Philip Ramsey, Junior."

Wendy walked to Squirt and knelt at his level. "Hi, there," she said. "You look like a pretty sweet guy to me."

A smile spread across Squirt's face as Wendy spoke to him.

"Well, most of the time he is," Becca admitted. "He's just being a little difficult today."

"We all have difficult days, I guess," said Wendy, scooping Squirt into her arms as she straightened up. "Hey, is the Flip-ster on TV?"

"He's trying to save someone's life, as usual," I filled her in.

"Cool," said Wendy. "We don't get cable. I love Flipper. He is one way cool dolphin."

Becca sidled up to Wendy and pointed to a character on the screen. "See that boy? He got stuck in the Everglades and Flipper is trying to get help," she explained.

"Your nose is red from the cold, Wendy," I noticed. "Want some hot chocolate?"

"I do!" Becca shouted.

"Sure, if you're going to make it," said Wendy. "I'll watch Flipper with these guys."

I was glad for the break and felt fine about leaving Wendy in charge. The kids had taken to her instantly. To me it proved that she really was the nice person I thought she was. I think little kids (and animals) are good instinctive judges of people.

I put three mugs of chocolate milk into the microwave and set it for two minutes. When the microwave beeped, I put the mugs on a tray and carried them into the living room.

Wendy was lying on her back, holding Squirt over her head. He was giggling helplessly.

"Do you think Flipper will get help in time?" she was asking Becca, who was sitting cross-legged on the floor beside her.

"He usually does," Becca answered seriously.

I handed out the mugs of hot chocolate and we finished watching the end of the show. Just as the credits were rolling, Aunt Cecelia came home. "Seems like everything is calm here," she said happily.

"All under control," I replied. (Good thing she hadn't walked in earlier.) Then I introduced Wendy to Aunt Cecelia.

"Are you a Baby-sitters Club member, too?" Aunt Cecelia asked her.

Wendy looked confused. "No. What's that?"

"You remember," I said. "My club I told you about."

"Oh, right," she replied, her face brightening. "No, I'm not a member. But I love to baby-sit. I do it all the time."

"You do?" I asked.

"Sure. I like kids."

I could tell it was true. She had certainly settled Becca and Squirt down.

With Aunt Cecelia back in charge, Wendy and I went upstairs to my room. We listened to my new CDs and talked about school. We also talked about horse books. It turns out that Wendy likes them as much as I (and Mal) do. But she hadn't read any horse books by our favorite author, Marguerite Henry, so I lent her a few.

The time passed quickly, and soon Wendy had to leave for supper. As I said good-bye, I realized I'd just spent the most relaxing hour and a half that I'd had in days. I was glad my busy schedule still allowed time for a new friend.

CHAPTER 2

"I'm sorry, the meeting hasn't really started yet." Kristy Thomas was speaking into the phone as I walked into Claudia Kishi's bedroom for the Monday BSC meeting. "I can call you back in five minutes when it does. Okay. 'Bye."

"Who was that?" asked Claudia, who was using her teeth to tear open a bag of potato chips.

"Mrs. Wilder," Kristy replied. "But I told her I couldn't talk until the meeting started."

"Wow!" I said. "The phone has started ringing already?"

With a loud crinkle, Claudia's potato chip bag split open. She offered the chips to Kristy and me. "I guess summer is really over," she commented. "Everyone is back to PTA meetings and working overtime and being busy."

Cradling a handful of potato chips, I settled onto the floor in my usual spot. "Were you guys so busy this time last year?" I asked.

Kristy pushed back the brim of her baseball cap and leaned forward in Claudia's director's chair. (That's Kristy's usual spot.) "No, but our business has grown a lot. We're really well known now."

The fact that the Baby-sitters Club is such a big success is largely due to Kristy. For one thing, she thought of the club. The idea came to her one afternoon when she was in the seventh grade. Her mother needed a baby-sitter for her younger brother David Michael. Kristy and her two older brothers, Sam and Charlie, were busy, so they couldn't sit. (Kristy's father wasn't around. He walked out on the family not long after David Michael was born.) So Mrs. Thomas was going crazy as she called a zillion numbers trying to find an available baby-sitter.

That's when Kristy was struck with her great idea. What if her mother could call only one number and get in touch with a whole bunch of sitters? That would be so convenient. Parents would love it!

Kristy told her idea to her best friend Mary Anne Spier and they decided to form the Baby-sitters Club. Claudia joined them, which was great. Not only is Claudia a terrific baby-sitter and a fun person, she also has her own telephone and her own telephone number. That

13

made it possible for people to call the BSC without tying up the main family telephone.

Kristy, Mary Anne, and Claudia weren't sure they had found enough members for a club, though, so they invited Stacey McGill to join. The four of them handed out fliers and put up signs advertising their new service. Parents wanting a baby-sitter could call Claudia's number between five-thirty and six every Monday, Wednesday, and Friday and reach four capable sitters at once. The business was an instant success!

Then Mary Anne became friends with Dawn Schafer and she joined. Mallory and I joined next.

Kristy didn't stop with one great idea. They just kept coming. She was the one who thought of the BSC record book, which keeps all our appointments straight, and she thought of the BSC notebook, which is full of information, advice, and entries about our sitting clients. (It's very helpful if you're going into a new job to know a little about the kids in advance.) Kristy also thought up Kid-Kits, which are boxes filled with small toys, crayons, coloring books, and other odds and ends kids might like. They are a real hit with the kids we sit for (all kids like to play with new stuff) and make us very popular baby-sitters.

14

If I were to list all Kristy's great ideas, the list would take up pages. She's a real dynamo. That's why she's the club president. The funny thing is, Kristy doesn't look dynamic. She's petite with shoulder-length brown hair and brown eyes. Most of the time she dresses in jeans and a sweatshirt. (She couldn't care less about fashion.)

However, nothing about Kristy is average. You'd know it within minutes of meeting her. Your first clue would be her big mouth. Kristy is very direct. (Some might even call her loud and bossy.) Kristy knows this about herself, but she doesn't care. That's how she is — take her or leave her — which is one of the things I admire about her.

One thing you'd *never* guess when you first meet Kristy is that she's rich. Her stepdad Watson is a millionaire! Her mom married Watson not long ago and Kristy's life changed in a big way! For starters, she moved across town to live in Watson's mansion. Now her brother Charlie has to drive her to club meetings. Her family also grew. She became an instant big sister to Watson's son and daughter from his first marriage, Andrew and Karen. (Although they are only at Kristy's house on weekends, some holidays, and part of the summer, Kristy has grown very close to them.) Then her mom and Watson adopted a Vietnamese girl named Emily Michelle who is now two and a half. And last but not least, Kristy's grandmother came to live with them to help take care of Emily Michelle. Add a dog, a cat, and two goldfish to the list and you have one big household. Come to think of it, it's a good thing they *do* live in a mansion!

Kristy checked Claudia's digital alarm clock. It said 5:27. "Where is everybody?" she grumbled.

"They still have three minutes," I said brightly. Kristy is what Aunt Cecelia calls *a stickler for punctuality* — which means she insists that every BSC meeting start at five-thirty *sharp*. And I do mean *sharp*! You should see the steely Look she gives you if you are even a minute late! It's withering. All the members live in dread of getting one. Everyone tries like crazy to be on time.

On Mondays and Wednesdays it's easy for me to be on time. I stroll in nice and early. But the Friday meetings are killers. On Fridays I have ballet lessons. Every Friday at the end of class I undress in a flash, race down the stairs of the school, and jump into Daddy's waiting car. All the way from Stamford (where my ballet school is located) to Stoneybrook I *pray* that traffic isn't too bad and that we make all the lights. Mostly, I arrive at the meeting on time, but I've received the Look on more than one Friday.

Five-twenty-eight. Usually everyone had reached Claudia's by now.

"Stop worrying, Kristy," said Claud. "They'll all get here." Even though she is the vice president, (mostly because we use her room and phone) Claudia isn't concerned about lateness. As Kristy was busy fretting over where everyone could be, Claudia was rummaging in the bottom drawer of her bureau. Just as I expected, she was looking for more junk food. "There you are," she said, holding up a pack of frosted cupcakes.

Claudia's bedroom reminds me of a big puzzle where you have to find the hidden junk food. It's stashed everywhere! Claudia has a weakness for it, but her parents don't approve, so she hides it. (They don't approve of her reading Nancy Drew books, either. So those are also hidden around the room.)

Since Claudia is such a junk food lover, it's a good thing she's someone who can eat and eat and never gain weight. Despite all the junk, Claudia has a model's figure. In fact, I think Claudia is gorgeous. She has long, silky black hair, beautiful, clear skin, and dark almond eyes. (She's Japanese-American.) Not only does she have natural beauty, but she has a unique fashion sense that really works to set off her good looks. For example, today she was wearing an oversized white shirt under a black vest covered with a design of shiny beads. (She sewed the beads on it herself.) She wore neon green leggings and black ballet slippers (on which she'd sewn a matching bead design). From one of her pierced ears hung a dangling earring made from the same beads and on the other ear she wore a small green hoop earring. It was an original look that only Claudia could make work.

Claudia is not only creative about her clothing, but she's creative in other ways, too. She paints, sews, does pottery, calligraphy, and sculpts. If it's creative, Claudia does it.

She is completely disinterested in school. I think that's because she would much rather be doing her artistic things. Or maybe it's because she wants to be different from her sixteen-year-old sister, Janine, who is a real-life genius. Whatever the reason, Claudia only does enough schoolwork to squeak by.

Claudia bit into her cupcake. "Anyone want some?" she offered through a mumble-mouth of chocolate.

"No thanks," said Kristy. "It's five-twenty-nine. I don't understand this."

Just then, Stacey McGill walked in and instantly checked the clock. A smile spread across her face. "All right!" she cried. "Made it!" She tossed her school backpack on the floor and sat on Claudia's bed. "I was sitting for the Arnold twins and Mrs. Arnold was late getting home. I couldn't be mad at her, though. As it was, she came home with wet hair. Her perm took longer than she expected. Perms can be a pain."

Stacey knows about perms since she wears her shoulder-length blonde hair in one. She's very pretty and has the biggest blue eyes. Like Claudia, she also has a great fashion sense, although her clothing isn't as "unique" as Claudia's. Claudia and Stacey are definitely the two most sophisticated members of the club.

Stacey is smart, too, a real math whiz. She's the club treasurer, which means she collects the club dues and budgets the money so that we can help pay Claudia's phone bill, pay Kristy's brother to drive her to meetings, and resupply our Kid-Kits. She's so good with budgeting that occasionally there's even money left over for something fun like a pizza party or a trip to the movies.

It would seem that Stacey has everything going for her, but she's had more than her share of problems. For one thing, she's a diabetic. That means her body can't regulate the amount of sugar in her bloodstream. She has to eat a healthy diet, no sweets, and she has to give herself injections of insulin each day. (She says she's used to giving herself the shots. I don't think I would ever get used to *that*!) Stacey takes it seriously because she has to. If she doesn't, she could faint or even go into a coma.

Stacey has also moved around a lot. She's originally from New York City. (Home of the New York City Ballet and the American Ballet Theater! If I lived there I think I'd love it as much as Stacey does.) Her family moved to Stoneybrook when her father's business trans-ferred him here. Then, just when Stacey had adjusted to the change, the company trans-ferred Mr. McGill back to the city. And then, shortly after the move, her parents split up and Stacey came back to Stoneybrook with her mother. (Here's something funny: My family moved into Stacey's old house!) Stacey is what my dad would call "a survivor." She has the ability to meet every challenge and make the best of it. She's got a pretty sunny personality.

Five-thirty! The moment had arrived.

"This meeting is about to begin," Kristy announced as she always did at the stroke of five-thirty.

Just in time, Mary Anne Spier skidded breathlessly into the room. "Thank goodness," she panted, looking at the clock. "I sat for Jackie Rodowsky today and he was more accident prone than ever. Just as I was rushing out the door to get here, he knocked over a huge bottle of root beer. It sprayed all over the place. I just *had* to help Mrs. Rodowsky clean it up."

That's Mary Anne for you! She's so nice she could never let Mrs. Rodowsky clean up alone. I think Mary Anne is one of the gentlest, kindest people I've ever met. She's a great listener who cares deeply about people and cries easily. She's very sensitive, *and* very organized.

Mary Anne is the club secretary, and no one could be better at it. She keeps up the club record book, which contains the schedules of every single club member. (Things like my ballet classes, Claudia's art classes, and Stacey's visits with her dad are all in there.) That way, Mary Anne knows who is free to take a babysitting job.

Mary Anne is Dawn's stepsister. Even before they were stepsisters, they were best friends. They're close as can be, but very different from one another. Unlike Dawn, who is tall with long blonde hair, Mary Anne is short and dark-haired. (Not long ago, she got her shoulder length brown hair cut into a very stylish short cut.) Dawn is a real health-food lover, but Mary Anne can't stand the taste of tofu or bean sprouts. She eats regular food.

21

Here's the story of how they became step-sisters, which I promised to tell you. One day Mary Anne and Dawn were looking through Dawn's mom's old high school yearbooks and they made an amazing discovery. Dawn's mom and Mary Anne's dad had been boyfriend and girlfriend in high school. But Dawn's mom went out to California to college and met Mr. Schafer, so, obviously, she and Mr. Spier never married. Now things were different, though. Mrs. Schafer was divorced and Mr. Spier was a widower. (Mrs. Spier died when Mary Anne was little.) Dawn and Mary Anne tried like anything to get their parents back together, and it worked! Well, not immediately, but after a lot of dating, their parents got married and moved into the old farmhouse Mrs. Schafer owned. (It is the coolest old place. It actually has a secret passageway that runs from Dawn's bedroom to an old barn out back. It was part of the Underground Railroad at one time.)

Mary Anne is pretty sad about Dawn's leaving. Even though she knows Dawn needs to spend time with her dad and her brother, I think the separation is hard on her. For the time being, she's lost a stepsister *and* a best friend.

Another thing about Mary Anne is that she's

the only member of the club who has a steady boyfriend. His name is Logan Bruno. He's this wonderful guy who is originally from Kentucky so he has a neat southern accent. Logan is an associate member of the club. That means he doesn't come to meetings, but we call him if no one else is available to baby-sit, or if somebody gets sick.

Shannon Kilbourne is our other associate member. She lives near Kristy and goes to a private school. We don't know her all that well, but everyone likes her.

Since Dawn left, we had been calling Shannon and Logan more than ever before. Unfortunately, Shannon was super busy with her school's honor society and wasn't available as often as she used to be.

Speaking of people who were not around, I wondered where Mallory could be. She's very responsible and it wasn't like her not to show up without even calling.

"Is Mallory sick?" Kristy asked me.

"She was in school today," I replied. "But she said she was feeling really tired. Want me to call her house?"

"I'm here! I'm here!" said Mallory, trudging into the room. "Sorry I'm late. Sorry, sorry, sorry." Her sorries didn't stop Kristy from giving her the Look, but Mallory didn't seem to care. She just plopped on the floor beside me. "I fell asleep as soon as I got home from school and I overslept."

"Are you feeling all right?" Mary Anne asked. "Maybe you're getting sick."

"Nothing hurts," said Mal. "It's just that I'm so tired."

"Everybody's tired since Dawn left," said Stacey. "We've all been baby-sitting too much."

"Maybe that's it," Mallory said dully.

I was concerned. I'd never seen Mallory so dragged out before. As I've told you, she's my very best friend, even though, at first glance, we don't seem to have much in common. The first thing that hits some people is the color difference. I'm black, and Mallory is very fair, with curly red hair. She wears glasses and braces and I don't. While I love to be physically active (especially when it comes to ballet), Mallory hates all sports (except for archery).

One thing we do have in common is our love of reading. As I've mentioned, horse books are our favorite. We also love to baby-sit, and were thrilled when we were invited to become junior BSC members.

Before she even took her first job, Mallory was a natural baby-sitter. Being the oldest of eight siblings means she's been dealing with younger kids all her life. Her experience, combined with her wild imagination (she wants to write and illustrate children's books when she grows up) make her a terrific baby-sitter.

"It's pretty clear to me that we have a problem," Kristy said in her usual get-to-the-point way. "Every one of us is running late or oversleeping because we have too much to do. We're trying to fit too much in."

"Should we find someone to replace Dawn?" Stacey asked.

Kristy rested her chin pensively on her fingertips. "I'm not sure. I'd like an alternate officer, though."

Dawn's job as alternate officer meant she could take over the duties of anyone who had to miss a meeting. She'd done every job at least once.

"On the other hand," Kristy continued, "what will happen to the new member when Dawn returns? Seven main members is plenty. Eight would be too many. We can't just ask someone to leave in six months."

"That's true, but we can't keep up like this," said Claudia.

"Maybe we've just had a very busy week," Mary Anne said. "Things might not be so hectic by next — "

She was cut off by the sound of the ringing phone. "Baby-sitters Club," Claudia answered. "Oh, hi, Mrs. Wilder. Yes, the meeting is on now. We were just about to call you back." As she spoke, Claudia grabbed a long yellow pad from her desk and began writing down the information Mrs. Wilder was giving her. "Okay, I'll check it out and someone will get back to you right away," she told Mrs. Wilder. Then she hung up and looked at Mary Anne who already had the record book open. "Mrs. Wilder needs someone to sit for Rosie from seven to nine next Saturday night," Claudia reported.

Mary Anne scanned the book as she spoke. "You're free, Claudia and so is . . . so is . . . no one. You're it, Claudia."

Claudia nodded. "Okay, I like Rosie now, even though she was a bit much at first. I guess since I live with a genius, I can understand Rosie." (Rosie Wilder is very precocious and she knows it, although I think she's funny.)

The phone rang again. It was Dr. Johanssen wanting someone to sit for Charlotte. I took that job since it was on Sunday afternoon. Becca likes Charlotte so she could come with me and it would be an easy job.

From that call on, the phone never stopped ringing. It was unbelievable — as if everyone in all of Stoneybrook was suddenly on the move, going here, there, and everywhere! The club members were all busy, either answering the phone, writing in the notebook, or discussing who was free to sit when. The movement in the room reminded me of a beehive with every busy bee buzzing around.

The only one not buzzing was Mal. She had propped herself against the side of Claudia's bed and fallen asleep.

CHAPTER 3

"Yes . . . sure . . . I'll get back to you on that . . . no . . . yes . . . everything's fine, it's just that we're pretty busy right now. . . . Okay, I'll call you back." Kristy put down the phone and sighed. It was our Wednesday meeting and things were nuts! "That was Mrs. Papadakis," Kristy said to Mary Anne. "She needs someone for — "

Before she could say another word, the phone rang again. "Baby-sitters Club," Stacey answered while Kristy consulted with Mary Anne about who could sit for Mrs. Papadakis. "Oh, hi, Mr. Hill," Stacey said. "Okay . . . I'll call you right back. 'Bye."

I sat on the floor paying attention to what was going on, but I also had one eye on the door. That's because I was waiting for Mallory. It was five-forty, and again, Mallory was late and hadn't called.

"Norman and Sarah Hill, seven o'clock this Friday," Stacey sang out.

"Hold on," said Mary Anne. "I'm still working on the Papadakises. No one is available."

"Call Logan," Kristy told Stacey.

"About the Papadakises or the Hills?" Stacey asked.

Kristy knit her brow thoughtfully. "The Papadakises — and then keep Logan on the line until we figure out if we need him for the Hills."

"Okay." Stacey had her hand on the phone to call Logan when the phone rang again. "Baby-sitters Club," she answered. "Hi, Mrs. Kuhn. . . . That's probably okay. I'll have to call you back, though." She hung up and began writing on her pad. "Jake, Laurel, and Patsy Kuhn, this Thursday at six-thirty," she called to Mary Anne.

"That's when Mrs. Papadakis needs a sitter," Mary Anne told her.

"So?" Stacey said.

"I already told you, no one is available then."

"You did?" said Stacey.

"Yes, she did. Don't you remember? You were supposed to be calling Logan," said Claudia as she sat cross-legged on her bed and wrote in the club notebook.

"Oh, right," said Stacey. She looked at her pad. "When did I say Mr. Hill needed a sitter?"

No one answered. "Didn't you write it down?" I asked.

"I didn't get the chance," she said with a sigh. "Darn, now I'll have to call him back." Stacey was about to punch in Mr. Hill's number when the phone rang again. "Baby-sitters Club. . . . Oh, Mallory! Where are you?"

I studied Stacey's expression as she spoke to Mallory. She looked serious and kept nodding her head. "Okay . . . uh-huh . . . gee . . . okay . . . I'll tell everyone."

"What?" I asked as soon as she hung up. "What's wrong?"

"Mallory says she's so exhausted that she just can't make it." Stacey told us all. "She says Mary Anne shouldn't schedule any jobs for her in case she's getting sick."

Now I was really worried. Mallory had looked pale in school, but she insisted that she didn't have a sore throat, not even a headache. Why was she so tired? It had to be something more serious than too much baby-sitting.

"Oh great!" cried Kristy, flinging her arms into the air in exasperation. "Now we're *two* members short."

"Poor Mallory," said Mary Anne. "I hope it's not serious."

30

"I care about Mallory, too," Kristy cried. "But this is a disaster!"

"Stay cool," Claudia advised. "Stacey, call Logan."

Stacey did, but Logan wasn't home. Next she tried Shannon. She was available, but obviously one person couldn't sit for both the Kuhns and the Papadakises at the same time.

"Send her to the Papadakises, and we'll try to get Logan for the Kuhns," Kristy advised.

Stacey said good-bye to Shannon and then called back Mrs. Papadakis.

"See, we'll work everything out," Claudia said hopefully.

"Mr. Hill!" Stacey cried, slapping her forehead. I forgot to call him back." She phoned Mr. Hill and got the baby-sitting information again. "Seven on Friday," she told Mary Anne.

Mary Anne studied the record book and then shook her head slowly. "Nope, no good. Everyone is busy."

"Ask Shannon," said Kristy.

Stacey called Shannon back, but she wasn't available.

"Now what do we do?" Kristy cried.

"If no one can sit, then no one can sit," Claudia said philosophically. "We'll just have to call Mr. Hill and tell him no one's available. It's not the end of the world."

"It *is* the end of the world!" Kristy disagreed with a frantic edge in her voice. "The whole *purpose* behind this club, the *idea* behind our business, is that when a client calls, he or she immediately gets a sitter. Anybody can call someone and *not* get a sitter. But when they call the BSC they are guaranteed to get a sitter every time! It's what makes us so pop — "

Once again, she was interrupted by the phone. "Sorry, Mrs. Kuhn, but I'm still working on it," Stacey said. "Yes, I realize you need to know. I'm really sorry but this is a very busy time for us with Dawn away. Someone will get back to you."

The phone rang *again*. This time Kristy snatched it up. "Baby-sitters Club. Hi, Mr. Hill. . . . No, I'm still working on it. . . . You do? Well, uh, um, that's all right. . . . Sure, I understand. But call us again and if something turns up for Friday I'll call you right away. I mean, just in case you haven't found another sitter yet. I'm sure someone will be available. I mean, we're working on it and we're hoping to hear from one of our associate sitters very shortly. All right. 'Bye."

"What did he say?" I asked.

"He said he can't wait for an answer and he'll have to start phoning some other sitters," Kristy said somberly. "This is *exactly* what I was afraid would happen. It's the worst possible thing. That's it! Enough is enough. We *have* to replace Dawn!"

"But what will we do when Dawn comes back?" asked Mary Anne.

"We'll worry about that then," Kristy replied. "Right now we have to do something. Anyone have any suggestions? Does anyone know someone who would be a good sitter?"

There was silence as each of us looked at the others. Suddenly, I thought of Wendy. I wasn't sure Kristy would want another junior member, but it was worth a try. "I know someone who's a good sitter," I said. "She's my age, but I think she — "

Just then the phone rang again. "Good, bring her to the next meeting," said Kristy before picking up the phone. Mrs. Barrett was calling. Dawn always liked sitting for the Barrett kids. She'd have jumped at the job. But Dawn wasn't here. "I'll have to get back to you," Kristy told Mrs. Barrett.

In the process of figuring out who could sit for Mrs. Barrett, Kristy forgot about looking for a new member. It turned out that Claudia had to take one of Stacey's jobs, so Stacey would be free to take the Barrett job. In order for Claudia to make that switch, I had to agree to take her afternoon job so that she could do her homework before going to the Barretts', because hardly anybody ever got any homework done at the Barretts' house. Those three kids keep you running.

The meeting was so confusing! Even the great organizer, Mary Anne, was starting to look frazzled. By the time we straightened out the Barrett job, it was almost six, but the phone rang yet again.

I decided to give everyone a break and I answered the phone myself. "Baby-sitters Club," I said in my most professional voice.

"Hi, it's me," said a lively, familiar voice.

"Dawn!" I cried, delighted to hear from her. "How are you? How is everything out there?"

As soon as I shouted out Dawn's name, everyone began to gather around me.

"It's great," Dawn replied. "I'm so glad I caught you. I raced all the way home from school so I could call before the meeting ended."

"You go to school until six?" I said.

"No, silly." She laughed. "We're on Pacific time. It's three hours earlier out here."

"I forgot," I said, embarrassed. "What have you been up to?"

"Lots of goofing off," she laughed. "It feels great to go to the beach again and to see Dad and Jeff. A lot of my old friends are in my class in school. Everything is great, but I miss you guys a lot. Are you all there?"

"Yeah, except for Mal. She's not feeling too

well. She says she's tired all the time."

"Oh, wow. That's too bad. Find out if she's taking vitamins. That might help her."

"All right. I'll ask her."

"How are you, Jessi?"

"I'm good," I said. "Feeling a little over-loaded, but basically all right."

"Listen, I'd like to talk more, but I'm paying for this call myself and I want to say hi to everyone. My baby-sitting money is running out. I need to find some sitting jobs out here."

"Too bad you're not *here*. We've got a ton of them," I told her. "Take care, Dawn. I'll put someone else on."

Everyone was anxious to talk to Dawn, but Kristy was right beside me so I handed her the phone.

That might have been a mistake.

"Dawn, you have to come home, like, right away," she said urgently into the phone. "No, I'm *not* kidding. We're in a mess here and we need you back."

"You're going to make her feel bad," said Mary Anne, reaching out to take the phone from Kristy.

Kristy turned away from Mary Anne, still talking into the phone. "Yes, that was Mary Anne. . . . No, you can't talk to her until you swear you'll come back right away."

Mary Anne reached around and scooped the

phone out of Kristy's hand. "Don't pay attention to her," she told Dawn. "We're doing all right."

"No, we're not!" Kristy shouted into the mouthpiece.

At ten after six, Claudia was talking to Dawn, with Stacey hanging onto the phone next to her. "We really miss you," Claudia said.

"We sure do," Stacey spoke up.

Silently I waved good-bye to my friends as I scooped up my jacket and walked out of the room. I was excited about the idea of Wendy joining the club, but I was also sad about the idea of trying to replace Dawn — as if anyone could.

CHAPTER 4

Thursday

I don't know what's the matter with me! I can't keep my eyes open lately. I thought I was feeling a little better until I tried sitting for the seven Pike maniacs. Maybe I've been bitten by some rare sleep causing bug who flew in from a strange tropical island.

I don't know what you're complaining about, Mal. I did all the work!

Rare tropical bugs! That's Mal and her runaway imagination for you. But, in truth, it was beginning to sound possible to me. What else could be causing Mal's mystery fatigue?

Mal and I sat for her younger brothers and sisters the next day, Thursday. She hadn't been in school so, when I arrived at her house, I was relieved to discover that she wasn't seriously sick. But, to tell the truth, she didn't look seriously well, either.

"Hi, Jessi." She greeted me dully at the front door as her mother rushed out the back door. She was wearing a faded lavender sweat outfit, her blue terrycloth robe thrown over it. "Come on in."

"What's the matter with you?" I asked.

Mallory shrugged listlessly. "I don't have a fever, or a sore throat or anything. I'm just *so* tired. Mom let me stay home from school today because she thinks I'm coming down with something."

"It could be," I said. "Maybe your body is fighting a flu and it's taking all your energy."

"Maybe," Mallory agreed, flopping down on the living room couch.

"Where is everybody?" I asked.

"The monsters are in the rec room," she said, and I knew she meant her brothers, Nicky (who is eight), and the triplets, Byron,

Adam, and Jordan (they're ten). "Vanessa is playing Chutes and Ladders upstairs with Claire, I think, and Margo is in her room doing something, I don't know what." (Vanessa is nine, Claire is five, and Margo is seven.)

Just then, I sensed another presence. I looked up and saw Claire, dressed in a tiger costume. She was prowling down the stairs. She growled at me when I spotted her.

"Aughhh! A tiger! Save me!" I played along.

"I am Shere Khan, Lord of the Jungle," she told me in a menacing voice. From three steps off the floor, she pounced down into the living room — and banged her shin hard against a chest of drawers. "Ooooowww!" she cried, clutching her leg.

I ran to her. "Are you okay?"

"Ow! Ow! Ow!" she sang out in pain as her eyes filled with tears. I pushed up the leg of her tiger pants and examined her shin. Sure enough, a purple bruise was already starting to form. "Owwwwww!" she continued.

I looked at Mal, who was now sitting forward on the couch. "Could you get some ice?" I asked her. I'm afraid there was a little edge of annoyance in my voice. But after all, this was her sister and Mal wasn't actually dying or anything. I shouldn't have had to ask her for help.

"Oh, yeah, sure," Mal agreed. She got off

the couch as if she were in a slow motion film and walked into the kitchen.

By then Claire's cries had died down and she was just sniffling. "This is going to be my Halloween costume," she said, between sobs. "Isn't it cool?"

"Very cool," I said as Mal returned with ice wrapped in a towel.

I was pressing the ice against her bruise when suddenly the entire living room began to vibrate. I'm not kidding, the floor was actually shaking!

Suddenly Byron, Adam, Jordan, and Nicky bounced into the room on strange purple shoes that seemed to have springs on their bottoms.

"You're not supposed to use those in the house," said Mallory as she held tight to a shaking lamp. The boys ignored her and kept bouncing across the living room.

"Come on, guys," Mallory pleaded weakly.

"We're not hurting anything," Byron argued as he jumped in place like a human ball.

I expected Mallory to take action. As the oldest of eight kids, she's used to taking charge, and is not a bit shy about it. But not this time. She just shook her head and sighed. I could see I was going to have to take control. "Listen, you guys," I said. "You have to take those outside. Really. Something's going to get broken."

The boys boinged slightly up and down as they thought about this.

"Please," I asked.

It proved to be the magic word, because they started bouncing toward the hall closet and grabbing their jackets. "The Kangaroo Corps will continue maneuvers outside," Adam said gallantly.

"Thank goodness." Mallory sighed.

The pictures, vases, and knick-knacks rattled just a few seconds longer as the boys bounced out the front door, slamming it behind them.

No sooner had the door slammed than an anguished cry came from upstairs. Mal and I looked at one another in alarm. "What's Vanessa doing?" Mal asked Claire.

"Setting her hair," Claire replied.

"How dangerous could that be?" I asked. But another pained cry came from above us.

"You'd better go see what's the matter," Mallory said to me.

"Me?" I cried. "What about you?" Mallory gazed at the stairs with weary eyes as if I'd asked her to climb the Himalayas. She sighed a long, exaggerated sigh.

"Oh, all right," I grumbled, heading upstairs. "I'll go."

When I reached the head of the stairs I saw Vanessa standing in the bathroom with the door open. Her face was red with frustration and her mouth twisted into a grimace as she tried to pull an electric roller from her hair.

"Ouch," I said sympathetically. "How did you manage that? And what happened to Chutes and Ladders?"

Snarled around one roller were two others, their small spikey grippers entangled in Vanessa's fine brown hair. The result was that on one side Vanessa had springy curls, while the other side looked as if birds had been trying to build a nest in her hair.

"We finished our game," replied Vanessa. "And I'm going to a pizza birthday party today at five-thirty. I wanted to look nice, so I thought I'd try out Mom's electric rollers. She never uses them, and now I see why."

Gingerly, I tried to pick the hair out of the roller, but it was hopelessly tangled. "Ow! Careful!" Vanessa complained each time I tugged.

"I'm trying," I said, feeling frustrated myself. After several more minutes, I gave up. "I'm going to have to cut these out," I said apologetically.

"No!" Vanessa cried in horror. "You can't! It'll look awful!"

"It's up to you, but I can't think of anything else to do."

Vanessa studied herself in the mirror. "Oh, all right," she relented with a dismal, defeated sigh.

"Do you have a sharp pair of scissors?" I asked.

"Mallory does, but I don't know where they are."

I went to the top of the stairs and hollered down. "Mal! Where are your scissors?"

I waited for her answer but none came. I ran downstairs and discovered Mallory asleep on the couch with a book of fairy tales on her lap. She was *snoring*.

"Shhh," said Claire, who was sitting on the floor below her, coloring. "She fell asleep while she was reading me *The Three Bears*. I don't blame her. I think it's a very boring story, too."

My only choice was to awaken Mallory with gentle shakes. "Mal, Mal," I said. "Wake up."

Her eyes fluttered behind her glasses. "Huh? What?"

"Where are your scissors?" I asked.

She blinked hard and looked at me blankly, as if my question made no sense to her. Then she woke up more fully. "Margo was using them. I lent them to her," she mumbled sleepily.

I ran back upstairs and knocked on Margo's bedroom door. "Go away!" Margo shouted although she didn't sound upset.

"It's me, Jessi," I called to her. "Do you have Mallory's scissors?"

"Just a minute," she replied. A moment later the door opened a crack and Margo handed me out the scissors.

"What are you doing in there?" I asked.

"Playing," she answered.

"Are you all right?" I asked.

She nodded. "I'm fine."

"Okay, thank you for the scissors."

"You're welcome."

Vanessa and I went into the room she shares with Mallory and began working on her hair. "Don't cut too much," Vanessa kept fretting each time I took a careful snip. When I was done, her hair did look a bit choppy. "Now what am I going to do?" Vanessa wailed, peering at herself in the mirror.

"I know." I hopped off the bed and gathered up the short newly chopped strands of hair on Vanessa's right side. I braided them, tying the end with a rubber band that I took from the top of her dresser.

"Cute!" Vanessa said, smiling at herself. "Thanks, Jessi."

"No problem."

Back downstairs, I colored with Claire for

44

awhile as Mallory slumbered. Every so often I checked the backyard where the boys had taken off their bouncing shoes and were busy playing chicken, trying to knock each other off their shoulders and into the piles of leaves on the lawn.

After an hour I checked on Margo. "I'm still playing," she called, answering my knock without opening the door. It struck me as strange that she didn't come out, but she sounded fine so I let her be.

I returned to the living room in time to keep the boys from flinging their jackets all over the furniture as they came in from outside. However, Adam threw his on top of Mallory and she didn't even stir. But I suddenly had a new insight into why she might be so tired. Taking care of these kids all by yourself was — well, it was exhausting!

CHAPTER 5

If I think Fridays are usually a rush, this Friday was beyond belief. For starters, Mme Noelle (she's my ballet teacher) kept us in class an extra five minutes. And then traffic in Stamford was horrendous! To top it all off, I had offered to pick up Wendy and bring her to the meeting.

She wasn't quite ready when I finally arrived at her house. I tried not to be aggravated with her, but she just wasn't moving fast enough. If she were me, I would have been flying around the house like a nut trying to get ready.

Finally, though, we raced to the car and Daddy drove us to Claudia's. "Come on, hurry, hurry, hurry," I urged Wendy as she climbed out of the car.

"Okay, but what's the big deal if we're five minutes late?" Wendy asked.

"Five minutes!" I yelped. "I'm worried about being *half a second* late! Come on!" I grabbed Wendy's wrist and pulled her along the walk. Luckily, Claudia leaves the front door open on meeting days, so we didn't have to knock. Still holding onto Wendy, I ran inside and up the stairs.

Breathless, I burst into Claudia's bedroom. It was five-thirty on the dot!

"Meet Wendy Loesser everybody!" I said.

Wendy smiled a bit nervously. "Hi."

Everyone said hello and then I introduced my friends by name. Even though we go to the same school, they hadn't met Wendy. And Mal (who was at the meeting despite her droopy eyes) is in the same grade but doesn't have any classes with her. "Hi, Wendy," said Mal, stifling a yawn. "Jessi has told me a lot of nice stuff about you."

"Same here about you," Wendy said.

"You're pretty young, Wendy," said Kristy, being her usual blunt self. "Have you ever baby-sat before?"

"Sure," Wendy replied. "I have two younger sisters. They're six and eight. And my neighbor next door asks me to play with her two-year-old for a few hours while she sells stuff over the phone. Plus, I sit for two kids down the street so their parents can go out and have supper together sometimes."

"That sounds like good experience," said Stacey.

Just then, the phone rang. "Baby-sitters Club," Kristy said, answering it. "Hi, Mrs. Rodowsky." She noted Mrs. Rodowsky's information on her pad and hung up. "Now this is how we operate," she told Wendy.

Taking on an ultra official, chin-up posture, Kristy turned to Mary Anne for the demonstration. "Mary Anne, please consult your book. I need a sitter for next Tuesday at five o'clock at the Rodowsky residence." (Kristy was being so formal for Wendy's benefit that I had to work hard not to laugh.)

"Are you out of your mind?" Mary Anne cried.

Kristy's hands went to her hips as she scowled at Mary Anne. I was sure this wasn't the way she wanted her demonstration to go.

"I'm sorry," Mary Anne defended herself. "But that time slot filled up three days ago."

"Are our associates Logan and Shannon busy then, too?" Kristy asked, still very official.

"Yup, they're booked," Mary Anne said, nodding solemnly. "The only one free that day is Jessi, but she can't sit that late."

"Wait! Wait!" cried Claudia. "I'm supposed to sit for Mrs. Barrett on Tuesday from three until six. Why doesn't Jessi take *that* job, and then I'll be free to sit for the Rodowskys."

"I have an early ballet class. I couldn't get there until four-thirty," I explained.

"All right, come and take over for me then, and I'll have time to get to the Rodowskys' house by five," Claudia suggested.

I didn't really want to do that. It would mean I'd be baby-sitting every afternoon for the rest of next week. "Maybe Wendy could do that job?" I suggested.

Kristy shook her head forcefully. "Wendy isn't officially in the club yet," she said. "I have to ask her some questions and if she can answer them, then she has to go on a test job with another sitter."

"Oh, all right." I sighed. Everyone was working so hard. I had to do my part.

"Now, Wendy," Kristy said. "What would you do in case of a medical emergency?"

Wendy considered this for a moment. "Probably call my mother. If I couldn't reach her, I'd call nine-one-one."

"Right," said Kristy. "What information should you get from the parents before they leave the — "

Before Kristy could finish, the phone rang once more. It was Mrs. Braddock. She brought on another no-one-can-take-the-job crisis.

"Call Shannon or Logan!" Kristy said yet again.

Logan wasn't in, but Shannon could take the job.

"Now, where was I?" Kristy asked Wendy.

"You were talking about some kind of information or something," Wendy reminded her.

"Oh, yeah," said Kristy. "What do you need to find out before the parents leave the house?"

"Well, I guess you should find out where they'll be," Wendy said.

"Anything else?" Kristy probed.

Wendy chewed on her lower lip thoughtfully. "You should also ask about bedtimes and — "

The ringing phone cut off the rest of her answer. This time the caller was Dr. Johanssen wanting someone to sit for Charlotte. While the others were busy figuring that out, I asked Mal how she was feeling.

"Like a flat tire," she replied. "Thanks for all your help yesterday."

"That's okay," I said. "Did you ever find out what Margo was doing in her room?"

"Huh?"

"She was so secretive," I went on.

Mallory shrugged. "Who knows? She was

probably playing some goofy game and she didn't want anyone to make fun of her."

"Is every meeting as crazy as this?" Wendy asked.

"No, we're usually super organized. But since Dawn left for California we're short-handed. That's why we need you," I explained.

"Mallory, can you sit for the Arnolds tomorrow afternoon?" Mary Anne asked.

"I'd rather not," said Mallory. "I'm still feeling crummy. I don't think I'm up to it."

"What is the matter with you, anyway?" Kristy exploded.

"I don't know," Mallory said helplessly.

"You'd better go to a doctor and get better," Kristy told her. "I'm not trying to be mean, but we can't have two sitters out of commission."

"I could sit tomorrow," Wendy volunteered.

Kristy pressed her lips together and narrowed her eyes as she studied Wendy. For a moment, I thought she was going to say Wendy should take the job. But then she shook her head. "No, I can't let you. It would be irresponsible. No offense, Wendy, but we just don't know you well enough yet. We promise our clients sitters we *know* are reliable. Why don't you go with Jessi to the Barretts next Tuesday? That way she can tell us how you did and we can make a decision about letting you join the club. Okay?"

"Okay," Wendy agreed.

"I'll call Mrs. Barrett and make sure it's all right for you to come, and if it's all right for Jessi and you to relieve Claudia, so she can leave early for the Rodowskys," said Kristy to Wendy. "Then I'll call Mrs. Rodowsky and let her know who the sitter will be."

"We still need a sitter for Dr. Johanssen," Mary Anne reminded Kristy.

"I'll call Logan," Stacey volunteered, picking up the phone.

"He won't be home until six today," Mary Anne told Stacey. (She tends to know his schedule.)

Kristy called Mrs. Barrett and got her permission for Wendy and me to come over and relieve Claudia. The rest of the meeting was spent on the telephone. Kristy never got to finish asking Wendy her questions.

"So? Am I in the club?" Wendy asked me as my friends and I walked out of Claudia's house together.

"Not officially," I told her. "But I'm sure you'll do great at the Barretts'. And after that you will be a junior member of the BSC."

"Congratulations," Mallory told Wendy.

"Not yet," warned Stacey, who was walking

alongside us. "But I'm sure you'll be fine."

I waved good-bye as everyone went in their separate directions. Wendy walked with me a bit further. "Don't worry," I told her when we were alone. "You're as good as in."

CHAPTER 6

"New recruit, Wendy Loesser, reporting for duty," Wendy said with a salute and a smile when I opened the door to her on Tuesday at four-thirty.

I was already wearing my jacket. "Let's hurry, we're supposed to be there already," I said, rushing out the door.

Wendy had ridden over on her bike, so I grabbed mine from the side of the house and, side by side, we rode to the Barretts' house on Slate Street. At least we started out side-by-side, but I was in such a hurry, I soon pulled ahead. "Slow down," Wendy called to me as I pedaled hard, my head ducked against the wind.

"I can't," I called back to her. "We're late."

According to my watch, we arrived at the Barrett house at four-forty. When Claudia opened the door, she was already wearing *her* jacket, and she was anxious to get going. (I felt as if I were in some kind of strange baby-sitting relay race.) Claudia checked her watch. "I can still make it to the Rodowskys' by five, but I have to get out of here right now, okay?"

"Sure," I answered.

"I wrote down all the numbers you need. The list is on the kitchen table. Mrs. Barrett said not to bother giving the kids dinner, she'll do that. And Marnie napped so she won't be sleepy," said Claudia in a rush.

"Where are they?" I asked as I looked around the Barretts' sloppy house. Mr. and Mrs. Barrett are divorced and Mrs. Barrett is not much of a housekeeper. In fact, you could say she's totally disorganized, although personally she is as beautiful and pulled together as a fashion model.

"In the rec room," said Claudia. "Marnie is in her playpen but you'd better get her right away because Suzi can lift her out of it, which she does at every opportunity. She thinks the playpen is inhumane or something. Mrs. Barrett promised to be home by six, but you know her. She's never on time, so be prepared," said Claudia pulling open the front door.

"It's okay, I cleared it with my parents that I might be later than usual tonight. My dad will pick me up when I call him," I told her. "Have fun at the Rodowskys'."

Claudia had barely shut the door behind her

when we heard a crash and the sound of crying. Wendy and I raced to the rec room, following the sound.

We found five-year-old Suzi in tears lying flat beside a playpen which stood in the middle of the room. Blonde, curly-haired Marnie, who is a toddler, was sprawled beside Suzi, howling her lungs out.

Instantly, Wendy scooped up Marnie and comforted her.

"What happened?" I asked, kneeling next to Suzi. "What hurts?"

"My head," Suzi wailed. "I bumped my head on the floor."

"Is Marnie all right?" I asked Wendy while I rubbed Suzi's head.

"I think she's okay," said Wendy. "She doesn't have any bruises or cuts."

"She's just scared," Suzi said, brushing away her tears. "She rolled out of my arms when I fell over."

"Were you taking her out of the playpen?" I guessed.

Suzi nodded. "She wanted to come out. I could tell."

Just then, eight-year-old Buddy appeared in the doorway. "All this noise is driving me nuts!" he complained. "Did Suzi take Marnie out of the playpen again?"

"You be quiet!" yelled Suzi. "Marnie hates the playpen!"

"How do you know?" Buddy challenged her.

"She never makes the ham face in the playpen!"

"The ham face?" Wendy asked me.

"That's her happy face," Suzi explained.

Wendy looked at Marnie, who had just stopped crying. "Show me the ham face," she cooed, wrinkling up her nose at Marnie. "Let me see the ham face. Come on, please." At first, Marnie just stared at her. Wendy stuck out her lower lip. "I want the ham face."

Marni thought that was very funny. Her eyes grew wide, she wriggled her nose, and she smiled.

"That's the ham face!" Suzi cried out. "That's it!"

Wendy and I laughed. The ham face was contagious. Even Buddy smiled. "I know a good game," said Wendy. "Suzi, why don't you and Marnie go into the playpen and pretend you're lion cubs in the zoo."

"Hey, who is she?" Buddy demanded, pointing at Wendy.

"This is Wendy. She's going to help me baby-sit today," I replied. Then I introduced the kids to Wendy.

"Hi guys," she said to them. "Okay. How about that lion game?"

"I have a better idea," said Suzi excitedly. "I'll be the mother lion and Marnie can be my baby. The playpen could be our cave."

"Okay," Wendy agreed.

"I'll be a hunter!" cried Buddy enthusiastically. He held up his forefingers as if they were guns. "Pow! Pow! I shot the lions dead!"

"We are not dead!" Suzi yelled indignantly. "There are no hunters in this game. Besides, you know the rule, Buddy. No playing guns."

"That's Dawn's rule," he objected. "And Dawn's not here."

From reading Dawn's entries in the BSC notebook, I knew what they were talking about. Dawn forbids Buddy (or any of the kids she sits for) to play gun games. Guns are not toys, and killing isn't a funny thing. Dawn wants to make that clear.

"I like that rule," I said.

"Me, too," Wendy agreed. "Let's keep it."

Buddy frowned at us. Then his shoulders sagged. "Oh, all right. Is Dawn coming back?"

"Yes," I assured him. "She's just living with her dad and her brother for awhile."

"I miss her," said Suzi.

"I'm sure she misses you guys, too," I said.

"What if she forgets about us?" Suzi asked unhappily.

"She won't," I said, although I suspected it was something we were all a tiny bit worried about, whether or not we were willing to admit it.

"You could always write her a letter," Wendy suggested. "That would let her know you were thinking of her."

"Or we could send her a video of us!" Buddy exclaimed, lighting up with excitement. "We did that in school once. It was so cool!"

"Hey! I was just about to say that!" Suzi said. "No fair."

"I know the reason you both thought of it," I said. "Because it's a great idea! Do you have a camcorder?"

"No," Buddy admitted. "But I bet we could borrow one from someone. A lot of people have them."

"Maybe we can get all the kids Dawn baby-sits for together and put them in the video," I suggested.

"What a great idea! I don't know Dawn, but I bet she'd love that," Wendy said. "Anyone would."

"Yeah! Yeah!" Suzi cheered as she danced around the room. "We're going to put on a play for Dawn!"

"All the other BSC members will want to help," I said to Wendy. "This will be great."

"I want to play a lion," said Suzi.

"I guess we can fit in a lion role somehow," I said, laughing.

"Yippeeee!" Suzi began crawling around the room growling. Marnie crawled after her. Before I knew it, Wendy had organized a game of lion in the jungle. Buddy agreed not to be the hunter, but settled on playing a crocodile that wanted to eat the lions.

This sitting job turned out to be the opposite of the job I had shared with Mal. Unlike Mallory, Wendy did everything. She played with the kids, fixed snacks for them, and read them *The Enormous Crocodile*, by Roald Dahl, which she'd brought in her backpack.

This was a nice break — being able to sit back and let someone else take charge.

As soon as I returned home, I called Kristy. "She's wonderful!" I said before Kristy even asked. "Wendy is the best baby-sitter you could ask for."

"That's good," said Kristy cautiously. "I wish she were older so she could sit at night."

"But we've been given so many afternoon jobs lately," I pointed out. "If Mallory, Wendy, and I together could cover all of them, then everyone else would be more available in the evenings."

"You're right," Kristy agreed. "Terrific. The

60

three of you might even take over Dawn's job of alternate officer."

The idea of holding a real club office was exciting. "Which one of us?" I asked.

"You'd take turns," Kristy replied. "You could be alternating alternate officers."

I laughed at the sound of that but it made sense. It was very fair, and if the three of us learned all the jobs then we'd be ready to move to other club positions when we were old enough.

"Oh, and also," I remembered to tell Kristy, "Buddy Barrett came up with a super idea about sending a video featuring all the kids we sit for to Dawn."

"Cool," Kristy agreed, obviously impressed. "It's so cool that I wish I'd thought of it. We'll have to get all the kids together on a specific day, which won't be easy, but I bet we can pull it off."

I knew we could, too, now that Kristy's great problem-solving brain was on the case. "Good work, Jessi," Kristy said. "You really bailed us out of a tough spot."

"No problem," I replied. "I'm glad Wendy worked out. She's so nice, too. You'll like her as much as I do once you get to know her."

When I hung up I was bursting with good feeling. I'd brought a friend into the club, and helped the club out in the process. Solving this problem made me feel as if I'd contributed something special to the club.

I couldn't wait to call the rest of the BSC members and tell them about the video idea.

But first I had an even more important call to make. I had to phone Wendy and tell her the wonderful news. She was now an official member of the Baby-sitters Club!

CHAPTER 7

Thursday

Operation Dawn's Video is in full swing. The minute I walked into the Barretts' house, Suzi and Buddy pounced on me. They were disappointed that I didn't show up with a camcorder all ready to go. I told them there were just a few (to say the least) things we'd have to do first. This project is a great idea, but it's not going to be as simple as it sounds.

Mary Anne's baby-sitting job at the Barretts' turned into the first planning session for the video. As she said, Buddy and Suzi were raring to go the minute she walked in, but Mary Anne pointed out to them that they weren't exactly ready to begin.

"What kind of play do you want to perform?" she asked the kids. Buddy and Suzi looked at one another with puzzled expressions.

"A video video," said Suzi with a shrug of her shoulders. "You know, like Snow White and the Seven Zorbs."

"The seven what?" asked Mary Anne.

Buddy rolled his eyes. "She means dwarfs. She never says that right."

"I did so say it right!" Suzi yelled. "I said zorbs! The zorbs are Grumpy, Dopey, Bashful, Sleepy, Doc, Sneezy, and, um . . . and . . ."

Mary Anne started counting on her fingers. She couldn't come up with the seventh dwarf, either. "It doesn't matter. We'll think of his name later," she said. "That's a good idea."

"No, it's not," Buddy disagreed. "How about a play about Captain Planet? Dawn likes ecology stuff and Captain Planet and the Planeteers are always protecting the earth from polluters like Duke Nukem. She'd like that way better than a dumb old fairy tale."

"It is not dumb!" Suzi protested angrily. "It's no fair if you get your way. You always get your way. Think again, buckaroo!"

Mary Anne's eyebrows shot up in surprise. "What did you just say?"

"She heard that on a cartoon this morning," Buddy explained with another roll of his eyes. "She's been saying it all day. Every two minutes she says, 'Think again, buckaroo!' "

"Do not!" cried Suzi.

"Do so," Buddy countered.

"All right, all right. That's enough bickering," Mary Anne told them. "How about this? What if we do both?"

"What do you mean?" Suzi asked.

"We could put on Snow White with Captain Planet in the story," Mary Anne suggested. "He could be . . . the prince."

"Yes!" cried Buddy. "But he doesn't kiss Snow White, 'cause the Captain never kisses or any gross stuff like that. He could fly Snow White to a secret laboratory where he gives her a special formula to make her better. And the witch could poison Snow White with a disgusting radioactive apple."

"The zorbs could be special secret planeteers," added Suzi.

"Hey, I think we're onto something," Mary Anne said with a smile. "Next we have to cast the parts."

"What's that?" Suzi questioned.

"That's when you decide which person will play which part," Mary Anne explained. "And we'll need costumes. We'll have to write our own script and you'll have to learn your parts."

"Laurel Kuhn could be Doc," said Buddy, "since she's so smart and all."

"Carolyn and Marilyn Arnold could be a two-headed monster," said Suzi with a giggle, referring to eight-year-old twins.

"I don't think there is a two-headed monster in this play," Mary Anne said, laughing, as she went upstairs to check on Marnie, who was taking a nap.

"There could be," said Buddy, trailing up the stairs with Suzi after Mary Anne. "We could pretend a little alligator crawled into a polluted swamp and turned into a two-headed monster."

Mary Anne shook her head. "I don't think Marilyn and Carolyn would like that idea. Maybe they could take turns playing Snow White. That way two people could have the lead part."

"I want to be the witch," said Suzi. "She has the best part."

When Mary Anne reached the bedroom, sleepy-eyed Marnie was just sitting up in her crib. "Marnie is perfect for Dopey," Suzi pointed out.

Mary Anne smiled down at the two-year-old. "She's probably the only one who wouldn't mind playing that part," Mary Anne agreed.

Mary Anne lifted Marnie from her crib and felt to see if her diaper needed changing. It did. "Who do you want to be?" she asked Buddy.

"Captain Planet, of course," he said as if the answer should have been obvious.

Mary Anne finished changing Marnie's diaper. "I have an idea. Why don't we call Jessi. She's baby-sitting over at the Braddocks' right now. Haley and Matt could come over with Jessi and we could all work on the play together."

When Mary Anne called, I was thrilled to hear from her. I was anxious to get going on the video but I didn't know where to start. I had already told Matt and Haley (Matt is seven, and Haley is nine) that we were making a video and they were excited about it.

"But what about Matt?" Haley asked when I hung up and told the Braddocks the idea for the play. "What part can he play?"

Matt is deaf. Technically, he can speak, but since he's never heard a human voice, it's hard for him to reproduce the sound of it. Mostly, he prefers to communicate through sign language. "There will be plenty of nonspeaking parts," I told Haley. "Or Matt can sign, and you'll translate. It'll be fine."

The Braddock kids and I hurried to the Barretts'. When we arrived the living room was a whirlwind of construction paper, tape, and scissors.

"We're making costumes!" Suzi announced brightly. She held up a cone-shaped hat made of red construction paper with a roll of cotton glued around the brim. She plunked the hat on Marnie's head, bending her small ears over. "She looks just like Dopey in the movie!" Suzi cried in delight.

As Suzi spoke, Haley's hands moved rapidly as she signed to Matt everything that was being said.

"The Walt Disney movie isn't the only version of Snow White," Mary Anne told the kids.

"Huh?" Buddy said. "What do you mean?"

"The story has been around for a long time. The Brothers Grimm wrote down a lot of fairy tales, but they didn't make them all up. Some had been around for so long that no one knows who made them up," Mary Anne explained.

"Do you mean Walt Disney stole the

story!?" Suzi asked, horrified by the idea.

"No," Mary Anne answered, laughing. "He just took the story and told it in his own way. Really, the writers who worked for him did that, I guess."

"Hey, that's what we're doing!" Buddy said happily.

"That's right," I agreed. "What should we do?" I asked Mary Anne.

"We need you guys to help us make hats and help us come up with a script," said Mary Anne as she rolled another pointy red cone and glued its edges. "So far this is what we've come up with. The witch is a big polluter who wants to destroy the planet. She hates Snow White because she's in favor of a clean earth — which kind of fits. You know, keeping the snow white, and all."

"Don't eat the yellow snow!" Buddy cried out and then burst into giggles. Matt laughed, too, when Haley signed the joke for him.

Mary Anne worked hard not to smile. "Well, that is the basic idea, I suppose. Anyway, in our version, the witch can't stand Snow White for helping the planet, so she tries to get rid of her, just like in the real story."

"So she drops her in a polluted swamp!" Suzi put in.

"And she's attacked by a weird mutant two-headed monster," added Buddy. "But Swamp

Thing saves her because he's a good guy even though he's gross-looking."

"Can I be Swamp Thing?" Haley asked.

"Sure," Buddy agreed.

"Anyway," Mary Anne went on as Matt, Haley, and I began rolling red hats along with her, "Swamp Thing sends her to a forest where Snow White meets the Seven Zorbs."

"The what?" I asked.

"Zorbs!" Suzi said impatiently.

"We're calling the dwarfs 'zorbs' since Suzi prefers it that way," Mary Anne explained.

"Zorbs is funny," said Haley. "I like that."

"The zorbs are planeteers," Buddy said. "They're like a secret division. And when Snow White gets the radioactive apple they go out looking for Captain Planet, which is me."

"It sounds like you have it all figured out," I said. "You don't need any help."

"Yes, we do," Mary Anne insisted. "We have to write down what all the characters are actually going to say. So, let's start at the beginning. We can open with the witch in her royal chamber talking to her magic mirror. Now what should she say?"

"What a fine day." Haley volunteered the first line in a crackly, witchy voice as she signed what she was saying for Matt. "I think I'll pollute it. But first let me check up on that nerdy Snow White."

With her usual secretarial efficiency, Mary Anne wrote down everyone's ideas and little by little (with a lot of laughs and some bickering) our play was written. (And our zorb hats were made, too.)

"Now all we need is a camera and we're ready to go," said Buddy.

"Not exactly," Mary Anne disagreed. "We need more costumes, and props."

"I know!" I said excitedly. "Why don't we check out the party store downtown. They always have the weirdest, neatest stuff."

"Do they have radioactive apples?" Buddy asked.

"No, but I saw a whole bunch of wax fruit there," I recalled.

"They have lots of costume stuff for Halloween, too," Haley said. "I saw these long, claw nails. They'd be great for the witch. And Swamp Thing needs lots of green stuff hanging off him."

"All that costs money," Mary Anne reminded them.

"Do you think we could use some of the BSC money?" I asked her. "I mean, this is a club project."

"We'll have to ask Stacey," replied Mary Anne.

"I bet she'll say yes," I said, more excited than ever now. This was going to be great!

CHAPTER 8

"Mallory!" I cried in frustration. "What *is* the matter with you? Either go to a doctor or get better!"

We were standing in the front hall of her house while everyone else waited for us outside. Perhaps I should have been less impatient, but here it was Saturday and we were all set to go to the party store just the way we'd planned, and Mal was backing out on me. She said she was (I'm sure you can guess) too tired!

"My dad will still drive you guys like he promised," she said sheepishly. "Honest, though, if I go I'll just be dragging around. I won't be any help."

"Too bad you're not putting on *Sleeping Beauty*," said Vanessa as she came down the stairs. (She had braided the short ends of the hair I'd cut and tied them with a rainbow bow.) "We know who would get the lead role."

"Ha, ha, ha," said Mallory, unamused.

"I suppose she can play Sleepy, though," Vanessa went on.

"Only the kids are going to be in the video," I told Vanessa.

"Too bad," Vanessa teased. "Mallory is a natural for the part. Don't you think?"

"You're a riot, Vanessa," Mal said. "Listen, would you do me a favor?"

"What?" Vanessa asked.

"Would you go with Jessi and Mary Anne, instead of me? You know, just to keep an eye on Margo and Nicky."

"Which is what you were supposed to do, Mallory," I reminded her.

"It's not my fault!" Mal insisted.

I was torn. Normally I'm sympathetic when someone is sick. But I couldn't tell if she was really sick. There was nothing sick about her except this constant tiredness, which was starting to sound like an excuse to do nothing but lie around. Only, that wasn't like Mallory. She isn't a lie-around person.

Mary Anne stuck her head in the door. "Almost ready?" she asked.

"Mallory isn't coming," I told her.

"You'd better see a doctor," Mary Anne said. She frowned thoughtfully. "Do you think we should cancel the trip? We have a lot of kids to keep track of."

"Vanessa will watch Margo and Nicky," Mallory said, volunteering her sister. "Okay, Vanessa?"

"I guess so," said Vanessa.

Vanessa is at a funny age. At nine, she still needs a baby-sitter. But she's mature enough to be a big help.

"I suppose if Vanessa helps, it will be all right," Mary Anne agreed.

"Come on, Vanessa. See you, Mal. Get some sleep!" I said as we dashed out the front door. In the driveway, Mr. Pike was warming up one of the family station wagons. It wasn't freezing, but today was probably the coldest day we'd had so far, around forty degrees. Suzi Barrett and Margo Pike were jumping up and down to keep warm. Nicky Pike and Buddy Barrett were solving the same problem by chasing each other madly around the front lawn. We'd agreed to let the kids come with us to the party store since they were so excited about the video.

"All aboard the Pike Express," Mr. Pike called to us. We loaded into the car and were soon heading toward downtown Stoneybrook. "I'll be back in an hour," said Mr. Pike as we pulled up in front of Pembroke's Party Store.

"That sounds good," Mary Anne replied as she helped the kids out of the car.

"You mind Mary Anne and Jessi," Mr. Pike told Margo and Nicky.

"And me," said Vanessa.

"And mind Vanessa, too," added Mr. Pike.

As he pulled away from the curb, we split the kids into two groups. We wanted Vanessa, Margo, and Nicky in one group, but Buddy and Nicky wanted to stay together. So we put Buddy and Nicky in one group and Suzi, Margo, and Vanessa in the other. "Then how am I going to watch Nicky?" Vanessa protested.

"Just keep an eye on Margo," Mary Anne told her. "And Suzi."

I took the girls and Mary Anne took the boys. We were carrying thirty dollars which Stacey had given us from the club treasury. Mary Anne opened her wallet and handed me fifteen. "You pick out fifteen dollars worth of stuff and so will I," she said. "But let's meet up before we pay just in case we picked out the same things."

"Good idea," I agreed.

Pembroke's is almost as big as a supermarket. It's loaded with the greatest oddball stuff. In one aisle alone, we found green crêpe paper to wrap around Swamp Thing; a large red apple made of plastic (it was actually a bank, but no one would notice that); pointy rubber ears for the "zorbs"; and a blow-up palm tree. (We had decided that the zorbs lived in a rain forest.)

Each of the kids had also brought a little money to buy some personal costume item. Vanessa wanted to play the woodsman, and she found a peaked brown felt hat with a feather in it. Suzi picked out a black witch's hat. (Since it was so near Halloween, the store was full of them.) Margo was going to play Sneezy and she found a big red nose.

There was endless stuff to look at. The girls nearly lost their minds when they reached the party favor aisle. Besides all the little knick-knacks, there were trolls of every description. Apparently Vanessa is a big lover of trolls because she couldn't take her eyes off them. She had to examine the costumes the troll dolls wore, oohing, ahhing, and giggling over each one.

Vanessa was so entranced that she wasn't watching Margo. I was, though. And that's when I saw her do something I couldn't quite believe. With a furtive glance in both directions, she plucked a small ring with a troll on it from the shelf and stuffed it into the front pocket of her jeans.

I was stunned.

I didn't know what to do. Margo was such a sweet kid, I couldn't believe she had just shoplifted. In fact, I refused to believe it. I decided she'd just put the ring in her pocket for safekeeping until she was at the register to pay for it. Maybe it was a gift for Vanessa and she didn't want her sister to see it. The gift idea made sense to me, so I didn't say anything to her. I decided to wait and see what happened at the register.

I hurried the girls out of the party favor aisle and into the next one. There we hit the jackpot — everything anyone could need for various theme parties. *Snow White and the Seven Dwarfs* was one of the themes. We found a plastic Snow White wig, cardboard pictures of the Disney woodland animals, and a plastic woodsman's axe. When we were midway down the aisle, Mary Anne and the boys came walking up toward us.

"Look what I found!" Buddy Barrett shouted as he ran toward us, holding a box over his head. "It's a Captain Planet costume."

"That's great!" I said, taking the box from him. I winced when I saw the price tag. Ten dollars! "I don't know if we can afford this much for one costume," I said.

"No problem," Buddy replied. "Mom gave Suzi and me money to buy Halloween costumes for ourselves. I can be Captain Planet for Halloween."

"Good thinking," I said. "What are you going to be?" I asked Suzi.

"Since I have the hat, I might as well be a witch," Suzi answered. "But I want those scary fingernails Haley told us about."

While we were off in search of the finger-nails, I kept a sharp eye on Margo. She didn't take another thing, though, at least nothing I spotted.

Not much later, we all met at the cash register and checked our stuff through. Mary Anne and the boys had done well, too. They found plastic whistles for the zorbs, plastic rings for the zorb planeteers to use as power rings (when they touch their rings together, Captain Planet shows up) and a blue nylon cloak for Snow White.

Mary Anne checked her watch. "I can't believe we've been here for an hour already!" she cried. "The time flew!"

But the time dragged as we stood on line to pay for our stuff. Mary Anne and I were very aware that Mr. Pike was now outside in the car waiting for us and we didn't want him to have to wait too long. And it was hard for the kids to wait. They kept wandering off to look at things and we kept having to call them back.

Finally, it was our turn at the register. We nearly drove the cashier crazy as we sorted through our purchases trying to keep straight who was paying for what.

Not until everything was paid for and we were on our way out did I realize Margo hadn't paid for anything. So much for my gift theory.

I watched, feeling helpless, as she walked out of the store with the ring in her pocket. It wasn't as if the ring cost a fortune, but still, stealing is stealing and it's never all right. I didn't want to confront Margo in front of everyone, and Mr. Pike was waiting with the car running. I had no opportunity to say anything to her, so I kept my mouth shut — for the time being, anyway.

My moment came once we were back at the Pikes' house. Margo and I were the last ones out of the car. "Can I talk to you a minute, Margo?" I asked, laying my hand on her shoulder.

"Okay," she said. From my troubled expression, she seemed to know this was serious. "What's wrong?"

I waited until I was sure everyone was in the house. "Margo, I saw you take that ring from the store."

"What ring?"

"Margo," I said firmly. She knew I wasn't accepting her lie, because she hung her head and wouldn't look at me. "Listen, Margo, you're not a baby. Seven is old enough to know that stealing is wrong."

"Are you going to tell my parents?" she mumbled, still not looking at me.

"Not if you tell them first," I said, trying not to sound too harsh. "Why don't you tell them what you did. Then I won't have to tell them."

Margo looked up at me with sad, wide eyes. "All right. I'll tell them."

"Good for you," I said. "You'll feel better once you talk to them."

We went into the house and joined the others. Mrs. Pike was looking at the purchases that the kids were eagerly showing her. "Hi, where's Mal?" I said.

"She's upstairs," Mrs. Pike replied as she tried on the witch's fingernails.

Mary Anne and I ran upstairs and knocked on Mal's door. "Come in," she said listlessly.

Mallory was lying across her bed, paging through a book of Grimms' fairy tales. "I thought I could find some stuff that's not in the Disney version of Snow White," she said. "Those Grimm brothers had the right name, all right. They are grim. Their versions of the fairy tales are much creepier than the Disney versions."

"The Disney movies are scary enough for

me," said Mary Anne, sitting on the end of Mal's bed.

"How are you feeling?" I asked Mallory.

She shrugged. "You know."

Mary Anne left because she had to walk the Barrett kids home. When Mallory and I were alone I was tempted to tell her about Margo, but I decided against it. I'd told Margo I wouldn't tell her parents, and in some way it seemed to me that my promise meant I wouldn't tell anyone. Usually I don't keep things from Mallory, so not telling her this felt strange. But telling her would have been wrong, too. I was stuck with an uncomfortable feeling I didn't like at all. I just prayed Margo really would tell her parents.

CHAPTER 9

Last week everything had seemed so great. Wendy was in the club, and we were working on a great project — Dawn's video. This week was turning out to be a totally different story.

Things started going wrong at the Monday club meeting. For starters, I had the sinking feeling that Margo hadn't said anything to her parents about her shoplifting. I was sure Mallory would have mentioned it to me if Margo had confessed. Mal might even have been annoyed with me for not saying anything to her, but she would have said *something* about it.

Instead she just draped her arm across the end of Claudia's bed and rested her head on it. It was only 5:25 and from the look of her, I had serious doubts as to whether or not she could stay awake for the five minutes until the meeting began.

What was I going to do about Margo? I couldn't just let the problem go. That wouldn't have been right. This was very puzzling and upsetting.

I didn't have more than six minutes to worry about Margo, though. That was because at 5:31 I began worrying about something else. Wendy! She hadn't shown up for the meeting yet. Of course, she might walk in any minute, but I thought I'd made it clear how important punctuality was. This was the third time that she'd been late.

At 5:32, the phone began ringing nonstop just as it had during the last several meetings. The first job to come in was one Wendy would have been offered. In fact, she was the only one who *could* take it.

"What's with Wendy?" Kristy asked me. "Where is she?"

"I don't know," I had to admit. "She was in school today so I know she's not sick."

"She should have called," Kristy said, clearly annoyed.

What could I say? Even though *I* wasn't late, I felt kind of responsible for Wendy's lateness. "Maybe she had a baby-sitting job that ran over," I suggested.

Mary Anne checked the record book. "No, she isn't scheduled for a job today," she reported.

"I'll have to call Shannon," Kristy said crossly.

"Before you get on the phone, I'd like to use it," Mallory spoke up.

"Why?" asked Kristy.

"I have to go home," Mallory replied as she struggled to her feet. "I want to call my mother to come pick me up."

"You don't even feel well enough to walk home?" I asked in alarm.

Mallory shook her head.

"Mallory, when are you going to see a doctor?" Mary Anne asked.

"Tomorrow," Mallory told her. "I have an appointment tomorrow evening."

"Good," Stacey said. "I'm getting worried about you."

"Me, too. We all are," Claudia agreed.

Mallory made an anguished face and sighed. "To tell you the truth, *I'm* getting a little worried about me. Not only am I always tired, but I feel like my head is in a cloud. I forgot to ask if someone could baby-sit for my brothers and sisters tomorrow so my mother can take me to the doctor. If you guys hadn't said anything about it, I might have forgotten altogether."

Mary Anne checked her book. "Let me see. Jessi, I know you have ballet class . . ."

"Wait! Not tomorrow," I replied. "It was cancelled. So I can take the job. But we need another sitter, too." The standing rule at the

Pikes is that they want two sitters if five kids or more need watching.

Mary Anne shook her head as she looked at her book. "No one else is available except . . ."

"Wendy," I filled in dismally.

"And Wendy isn't here," added Kristy unnecessarily.

Mallory called her mother and then went downstairs to wait for her. "Gosh, I hope it isn't something serious," I said when she was gone.

"What if it's some terrible disease?" Claudia said in a hushed, serious voice.

"Don't let your imagination blow this up," Kristy warned. "She's probably just got some kind of flu or something. And I hope we don't all catch it. If we have to close up for a couple of weeks we might just have to close up for good."

What a horrible thought! "Why?" I asked.

"Because everyone will find other sitters," said Kristy. "And once that happens they'll stick with their new sitters. We haven't heard from the Hills once since we couldn't take that job last week."

"Maybe they haven't gone out since then," said Stacey hopefully.

"Maybe, but I don't like it," Kristy grumbled. "It makes me nervous. The Hills may not be our biggest customers, but I don't like to lose even a single client."

"I don't think we've lost them," Stacey insisted.

"We don't know," said Kristy glumly.

The phone rang again. The caller offered another afternoon job that Wendy could have taken. "Call Wendy's house," Kristy said, handing me the phone. "Please."

I called but no one answered. "I hope everything is all right," I said.

As the meeting wore on we wound up calling Shannon and Logan a lot. Wendy could have taken those jobs if she'd been there. Logan and Shannon filled some slots, but they couldn't take every job. By 5:55, we still hadn't found another sitter for the Pike job.

At that moment, Wendy burst into the room. "Hi, everybody," she said brightly.

"Where have you been?" Kristy demanded.

A look of bewilderment came over Wendy's face. I could see she didn't understand why Kristy had spoken so sharply. "I had a baby-sitting job, but the mother was late coming home," she explained. "Did any jobs come in for me?"

"Plenty. But you weren't here," Kristy told her.

I'm sure Wendy could see that Kristy was angry. But she didn't react the way I would have. I'd have been mortified and apologetic. Wendy grew angry in return.

"What's the big deal?" she asked. "Can't Mary Anne tell from that record book thing whether or not I'm free? Why do I have to be here?"

"Because you have to be," Kristy said, her face turning pink.

"We're all expected to come to every meeting unless we have an emergency," I explained.

"Well, this was an emergency," Wendy insisted. "I couldn't leave the kids by themselves."

"Next time, call," Mary Anne said mildly. "And why did you take a job without telling us?"

"What do you mean?" asked Wendy.

"That's the second club rule you've broken," Kristy jumped in.

"I don't know what you're talking about!" Wendy said irritably, her hands on her hips.

"First you were late without calling, then you took a job that wasn't offered to the rest of the club," Kristy said coolly.

"Are you saying I have to hand my regular jobs over to the club?!" Wendy cried indignantly.

"We all share jobs," said Stacey. "Even if a client asks for a certain sitter, we offer it to everyone in the club. That's the only way to be fair."

"Okay, I can see that, I guess," Wendy conceded reluctantly. "Sorry. And next time I'll call."

"Can you sit with Jessi at the Pikes' tomorrow after school?" Mary Anne asked her.

"Yeah, sure," Wendy said sulkily.

"Great," I said, trying to lighten the mood. "If you could be there a little early or at least exactly on time, that would be really helpful."

"Okay, okay," Wendy said testily.

The meeting ended then and Wendy didn't lose any time getting out of there. "Wait up," I called to her on the stairs.

She stopped and waited. "Sorry, Jessi," she said when I reached her. "I didn't mean to snap at you before. I was just ticked off. Who does Kristy think she is?"

"She's the president of the club," I said evenly. "If she wasn't strict, things wouldn't run nearly as efficiently as they do. Our customers wouldn't be as happy, and neither would we. It's better that Kristy makes everyone obey the rules."

"Does she have to be so crabby about it?" Wendy asked as we walked out into the chilly evening.

"She's just tense these days," I explained.

"I guess she thinks the club is in trouble."

As I spoke those words, the terrible reality of them hit me. It wasn't like Kristy to get excited over nothing. Maybe the club really *was* in trouble.

CHAPTER 10

The next day I hurried to Mal's house and arrived five minutes early. I looked around, expecting to see Wendy, and my heart sank. No Wendy. "Where is she?" I asked Mallory.

"She'll probably be here in a minute," Mal answered.

"I specifically asked her to be on time!" I exploded.

Mrs. Pike came into the living room with her coat on. "Hi, Jessi," she said. "Where's the other baby-sitter?"

"That's what I'd like to know," I blurted out.

A frown line creased Mrs. Pike's forehead as she checked her watch. "Oh, well, I suppose we can stay a few more minutes. There's always a wait at the doctor's office, anyway. But I don't want to miss the appointment. I called a week ago and this was the only time they had available. I don't want to have to wait another week."

. "Why don't you go," I suggested. "I'm sure Wendy will be here soon."

"But what if she's not?" Mrs. Pike fretted. "All the kids are here this afternoon. Seven is a lot to handle on your own, Jessi."

I knew she was right. Sometimes the Pike kids are as good as gold. And other times they seem to be going in seven different directions at the same time.

"How about this?" I said. "If she doesn't show up in fifteen minutes, I'll call someone else to come over. If I can't get anyone, I'll . . . I'll . . . I'll call Aunt Cecelia to come over with Becca and Squirt."

"I'd hate to ask her to do that," said Mrs. Pike.

I didn't like the idea myself, but I couldn't think of anything else. "She won't mind," I said, not quite sure that was true.

Mrs. Pike checked her watch again. "Oh, I suppose we really better get going. Dr. Dellenkamp's number is on the refrigerator. Mr. Pike will be home by six at the latest, but we should be back before then."

During this conversation, Mal had slumped onto the couch. If Mrs. Pike didn't get going soon, she was going to have to wake her up, or carry out a sleeping body. "Promise me you'll call someone if Wendy doesn't show up," Mrs. Pike went on anxiously.

"I promise," I said.

"All right then, come on Mallory," her mother said. "Let's get going." Mallory gave me a listless wave as she picked her jacket off a chair and trudged out the door behind her mother.

I went downstairs to the rec room and said hi to the boys who were playing a game of Nok Hockey. Then I headed upstairs where I found Vanessa lying on her bed doing homework and Claire putting together a picture puzzle on the floor at the foot of the bed. "Hi, guys. Where's Margo?" I asked.

"Hi. In her room," Vanessa replied.

"She made me come in here to do my puzzle," Claire complained.

What *was* Margo doing alone in her room all the time? I knocked on her door. Inside, I heard the sound of shuffling footsteps, but no one answered. "Margo?" I called. "It's Jessi. Are you all right?"

There was still no answer.

"Margo?" I wondered if I should just go in. Normally, I wouldn't, but I was beginning to worry. "Margo, if you don't open the door, I'm coming in," I called through the door.

Almost instantly the door cracked open. "Hi, Jessi. I was asleep."

I studied her face and decided she didn't look as if she'd just awakened. "Can I talk to you?" I asked.

"I'm pretty sleepy," Margo protested. "Can I just sleep another hour and then we'll talk?" As if to make her point, she yawned widely.

"I suppose that would be all right," I agreed. "But it's important."

"Okay, thanks," Margo said as she shut the door.

I hoped she didn't have whatever Mallory had. Or was this just a way to avoid talking to me?

By the time I was downstairs again, my fifteen-minute waiting period was nearly up. I went to the phone and punched in Wendy's number. "Is Wendy there?" I asked her mother.

"No, she's not. She had a baby-sitting job after school," her mother answered.

I wasn't sure if she meant *this* baby-sitting job or another one. I couldn't believe she would have just forgotten about sitting for the Pikes.

"If she comes in, would you ask her to call Jessi at Mallory's house?" I said.

Mrs. Loesser agreed to do that and I hung up the phone. Things were so calm that I was tempted to wait a while longer before calling anyone else. But I had made a promise to Mrs. Pike, so I had to start looking for another sitter.

But who?

Then I remembered that Mary Anne wasn't baby-sitting until seven-thirty that night. She wanted to keep the afternoon free to work on a paper. At least I knew for sure that she was home.

"Mary Anne? It's me, Jessi," I said when she picked up the phone. "I'm desperate. Wendy hasn't shown up. I need you to come over to the Pikes'."

"I can't," she said in a panicked voice. "I have to turn this paper in tomorrow. I thought I'd have all last week to work on it, but I wound up taking so many sitting jobs I didn't get to it. I really can't."

"Please," I begged.

For a moment there was silence on the line. "All right," Mary Anne finally said reluctantly. "But I'm going to sit in the kitchen and work. I can only be disturbed if it's an emergency."

"That's a deal," I agreed. "Thanks a million."

"Okay. I'll be right there."

Mary Anne arrived looking pretty frantic.

Four thick books were tucked under her arm and a pen was stuck behind her ear. "Sorry I was short on the phone," she apologized. "But this paper is one fourth of my grade and — "

"It's all right," I cut her off. "I appreciate that you came. Go into the kitchen and work. I won't bother you unless — "

At that moment we heard a knock at the door. I opened it and Wendy walked in. "Where have you been?" I asked.

She opened her mouth to speak, but then her eyes darted to Mary Anne and she seemed to think better of it. "Is everything all right?" Mary Anne asked her.

"Uh, yeah," said Wendy. "I had something to do at school and it went longer than I expected. I knew Jessi would be here so I didn't think it was a big deal."

"But Mrs. Pike asked for *two* sitters," I reminded her, my voice full of the exasperation I was feeling.

"I knew *you'd* get here on time," she said with a smile.

Mary Anne and I didn't smile back.

"I have to go home and finish this," said Mary Anne, taking her coat from the front hall closet and putting it on. "See you guys later," she said as she hurried out the door.

"I didn't want to say anything in front of

Mary Anne," Wendy told me when Mary Anne was gone, "but I didn't *really* have anything to do at school."

"Then why are you late?"

"My next door neighbor asked me to look after her baby because she had to do some phone selling. All of a sudden she hit a hot streak and people were ordering stuff like crazy from her. I couldn't just walk out on her, and, like I said, I knew you were here already."

"Wendy! You're not supposed to take jobs by yourself!" I cried. "Kristy told you that yesterday!"

"Nobody else knows this baby," Wendy insisted. "She won't go to just anybody. Besides, Mrs. Behar only asked me this morning as I was leaving for school. What was I supposed to do?"

"Well, I'm not exactly sure," I admitted. "I guess you should have told her no, or given her the number of our club."

"Oh, come on, Jessi," Wendy scoffed. "What harm did it do?"

"If all of us took our own private jobs we wouldn't have any club customers," I said.

Our argument was cut off by the sound of shouting in the rec room. When Wendy and I ran down there we found that an argument over Nok Hockey scoring had gotten out of hand.

"Hey, chill out, you guys," Wendy said, jumping into the middle of things, and catching a flying rubber dinosaur before it could smash into the wall behind her. "Now what's the problem?" she asked the boys.

"The problem is he's a cheater!" Jordan cried indignantly, pointing an accusing finger at Adam.

"You're a liar! That's the problem!" Adam shot back. "I didn't cheat."

Apparently Adam thought that he and Byron had earned the most points and Jordan thought he and Nicky were winning.

"It's hard to keep track of the score while you're playing," Wendy said diplomatically. "I say you should have a rematch and *I'll* keep score."

The boys agreed and Wendy pulled a stool up to the middle of the board. Realizing there was nothing further for me to do, I went upstairs.

For the next half hour, I read my social studies book. I got up once and checked the rec room. Wendy was busy playing Nok Hockey with Adam while Byron kept score. She *was* great with kids. There was no doubt about that.

I realized almost an hour had gone by since I'd spoken to Margo. It was time for me to have my talk with her.

But as I headed up the stairs, Mallory and her mom walked in the front door. "Hi. What did the doctor say?" I asked.

"That I'm okay," Mallory told me as she unzipped her jacket.

"Then why are you so tired?" I asked.

"She thinks Mal's rundown and might be riding out a virus," Mrs. Pike said. "She also thinks she might be a little anemic."

"She gave me these iron pills to take to make my blood redder or something like that," Mal said, holding up a small white bottle. "And she said to get some extra rest, eat healthy food, and do stuff like that."

"Great!" I said. "Boy, I'm glad it's nothing super serious."

"Well, she took some blood tests just to be sure, but she doesn't think I have anything to worry about," Mal said.

"Was everything all right?" Mrs. Pike asked me.

"Fine," I replied. "Wendy is downstairs with the boys, and everything is quiet with the girls upstairs."

"Terrific. Thank you, Jessi," said Mrs. Pike. She went into the kitchen, leaving Mal and me alone.

"I told you Wendy would come," said Mallory.

"Yeah," I replied absently, wondering how much I should tell her about Wendy's excuse for being late. I was also wondering if the time had come to talk to Mallory about Margo.

I had some serious thinking to do that night.

CHAPTER 11

The next day, Mal wasn't in school, so I stopped by her house afterward to see how she was feeling. Her condition was about the same, but her mood was a lot better. Seeing the doctor had made her feel sunnier about things.

"At least now I can relax and just rest because the doctor told me to," she said as she stretched out on her bed. "Before this I kept feeling like I should force myself to do things since I wasn't really sick."

We talked about Dawn's video and wondered how Dawn would feel when she got it. "Maybe it will make her homesick," said Mal.

"I hope not," I gasped.

"I hope *so*," Mallory disagreed. "Then maybe she'll come home sooner. It doesn't feel right without her around."

"I know what you mean," I said. At meetings I kept waiting for Dawn to speak up and give her opinion. I missed the way she could be so passionate about the things she thought were right. It was as if there were an empty space where she used to be and I wanted that empty space filled.

If Dawn were here, I might have asked her what she would do about Margo's shoplifting. But that wouldn't have been necessary. I already knew what she would do.

"Mal," I said. "I need to talk to you about something serious."

"What?"

"Has Margo mentioned anything to you or your parents about her . . . um . . . shoplifting?"

"Her what?!" Mallory cried out with more energy than I'd seen in days.

"Her shoplifting." I repeated. "I saw her take a ring from Pembroke's the other day."

"Without paying for it?" Mallory asked in disbelief. "Are you sure?"

"Yes. I even spoke to her about it. She said she'd tell your parents herself. Do you know if she has?"

"I don't think so," Mal said. "I'd know if something unusual was going on. Why didn't you tell me sooner?"

"Don't be mad," I said. "I didn't think it was right to give away Margo's secret."

"I can understand that, I guess," Mal said,

swinging her legs down to the floor. "But I think we better have a talk with Margo right now."

With Mal in the lead, we walked down the hall to Margo's room. "Margo!" Mallory called as she rapped sharply on the door. "I have to talk to you. It's important."

The door cracked open. "I'm busy," said Margo.

"Then get unbusy and come to my room," Mallory demanded. "If you're not there in two minutes, I'm coming back to get you."

Without waiting for an answer, Mallory turned and headed toward her own room. "You *are* feeling more like your old self," I commented.

"I can't imagine why she would steal from a store," said Mallory. "She knows that's wrong."

We sat in Mallory's room and waited another two or three minutes for Margo. "Okay, that's it, I'm going back in there to get her," Mallory said. But when she pulled her door open, Margo was standing there. I think she had been working up the nerve to come in. I suppose she'd guessed what Mallory wanted to talk to her about.

Margo stepped into the room looking pale, her eyes cast down at the rug.

"Margo, did you take a ring from Pembroke's without paying for it?" Mallory asked, getting right to the point.

A fat tear rolled down Margo's cheek and she nodded slightly.

I was a bit relieved. Things could have been pretty unpleasant if she'd denied it.

"You have to tell Mom," Mal said calmly.

Margo looked up for the first time since she'd walked in. Her eyes were wide with alarm. "I can't," she wailed.

"I'll help you," Mal offered. "Jessi will help, too."

"You will?" Margo said. "How?"

"All we can do is go with you," Mallory told her. "But then you won't be alone. We'll be by your side."

Margo sighed deeply. Her shoulders sagged and her head drooped. "All right. Let's go."

The three of us went downstairs and found Mrs. Pike in the kitchen making a big pan of ziti for supper.

"Mom," Mallory said, "Margo has to tell you something."

Mrs. Pike wiped her hands on a dish towel, and turned to Margo. "What is it?"

"Margo's voice was small and quivering. "I didn't mean to do it but I just sort of did anyway," she began.

Mrs. Pike sat down on a kitchen chair. "What did you do, sweetheart?"

"I stole something from Pembroke's," Margo said, bursting into tears as she spoke. "It was a ring, and the time before that I took two packs of gum and a rubber dinosaur." Covering her face with her hands, Margo began to sob deeply.

For a moment, no one spoke. The only sound was Margo's crying. Then Mrs. Pike pulled a paper napkin from a holder and handed it to Margo. "Why didn't you pay for those things?" she asked gently.

Margo wiped her eyes and shook her head. "I don't know. It was like a sort of game. I wanted to see if I could do it. They were my secret things that I could play with all alone."

I suddenly realized why Margo had been so secretive in her room lately. She was playing with her stolen treasures.

"You know that stealing is wrong," said Mrs. Pike. "Didn't that bother you?"

"Sort of," Margo admitted. "I figured I'd pay for the things some other time."

"When was that going to be?"

Margo shrugged. "I'm not sure," she mumbled.

"What do you want to do about this?" asked Mrs. Pike, laying her hands on Margo's shoulders.

"I don't know."

"Yes, you do," Mrs. Pike said softly.

"Return the things?" Margo asked. Her mother nodded. "But I can't," said Margo. "I've eaten all the gum."

"Then you'll have to pay for it," said Mrs. Pike. "Do you have any money?"

"Some, in my piggy bank."

"Go get it, then," Mrs. Pike told her. "We'll go over to the store right now."

"Now?" Margo wailed.

"I think we better."

"But . . . but . . ." Margo protested desperately. "Could Mallory and Jessi come with me?"

"Mallory is sick," Mrs. Pike replied. "Jessi, do you want to come?"

"I'll come. Sure," I agreed.

"Mallory, do you think you can get another sitter to come over while we're gone? We'll only be about an hour," Mrs. Pike said.

While Margo and I went upstairs and pried open her piggy bank, Mallory tried to find a sitter. Since Stacey lives in the house behind the Pikes, she was the first one Mallory called. "I have a sitting job at six-thirty," Stacey said. "But if you're sure your mom will be back soon, I can come."

Mallory assured her she'd be able to get to her job on time, so Stacey came over. "Hi, Jess," Stacey said as she came through the front door. "How come you can't sit?"

"It's a long story," I said. I didn't want to embarrass Margo by telling Stacey what was going on.

The drive downtown to Pembroke's seemed very long. No one spoke. Occasionally Margo sniffled. When we reached the store, Mrs. Pike asked to see the manager. We were directed to a small, plain office at the back corner of the store.

I felt sorry for Margo. She looked one hundred per cent miserable.

The manager's door was open and she invited us in. "May we speak to you?" Mrs. Pike asked the slim, dark-haired woman.

"Certainly," she said pleasantly.

"Margo," Mrs. Pike prompted.

Margo pulled the troll ring and the dinosaur out of her jacket pocket and laid them on the manager's desk. The manager just looked puzzled.

"I took these things. I'm sorry," Margo said in a small voice. "I also owe you money for two packs of gum."

"That's a dollar," the manager told her. Margo fished a handful of coins from her pocket and counted out a dollar. "Thank you," the manager said when Margo handed her the money, and Margo's eyes flooded once again.

"Young lady, I appreciate your making up for what you did," said the manager. "I wish more young people had that courage. You know, shoplifting hurts everyone. Stores have to make up for their losses by raising the price of everything. You've done the right thing." She paused. "I'm sure you'll never shoplift again."

"No, I won't," said Margo, wiping her eyes. This time I was sure she was telling the truth.

CHAPTER 12

"This is so cool!" Stacey said happily. "I feel like a real filmmaker." She held the camcorder to her eye and framed different shots of the Barretts' living room.

The big day had come at last. It was Saturday, the day we'd picked to film Dawn's video. With the help of the BSC members, the kids had been practicing all week long. Now they were ready for their performance. (Ready as they'd ever be, anyway.)

Mr. Braddock had donated his camcorder for the day and Mrs. Barrett had volunteered her living room as the set. In a flash, Stacey and I had run around and straightened up the Barrett clutter. We had pushed the furniture against the walls and draped sheets over it. The only piece we'd left out was a stuffed chair with a high back. We had decorated the arms and top with tin foil to make it look like a throne.

Now the kids were dressed in their costumes and ready to give the performance of a lifetime. (We hoped.)

"Act one, coming up," Stacey announced. "Is everybody ready? Queen?"

"Here I am," said Suzi Barrett, who was wearing her mother's dress, which was way too big for her, and a silver crown. She'd pulled her brown hair into a ponytail that bobbed up and down out of the middle of her crown. For the finishing touch, she'd painted her lips with bright red lipstick.

"Magic mirror, are you ready?" Stacey asked.

Adam Pike emerged from the kitchen holding a large wooden picture frame. He was dressed in a football jersey and jeans. "Adam, you're supposed to be wearing Dad's black robe. Didn't you remember?" asked Vanessa.

"I'm not wearing that robe!" Adam insisted. "It looks like a dress."

"Well, he can't wear *that*!" cried Suzi. "He doesn't look like a magic mirror."

"Yes, I do," Adam insisted. "How do you know what a magic mirror looks like?"

"Think again, buckaroo," said Suzi. "You do not look like a magic mirror."

"Come on, Adam," I pleaded. "You agreed to be the mirror. And what about your makeup?"

"Oh, all right!" Adam stomped huffily back into the kitchen. Moments later he returned wrapped in a black terrycloth robe that trailed behind him, his face smeared with green makeup.

"That's more like it," Suzi said with an approving nod.

"Quiet on the set, everybody!" Stacey yelled. Amazingly, everyone did quiet down. Suzi sat on the big chair and Adam stood, holding the picture frame.

"Okay, at the count of three I'm going to start filming," Stacey told them. "One, two, three, action!"

"What a lovely day," Suzi croaked in her witchiest voice. "I think I'll pollute it. I'll make a potion that covers the sky with clouds of yucky pollution."

She stood up and went to the magic mirror. "Magic Mirror on the wall — the one I bought at the Washington Mall. Who is the biggest polluter of all?"

"You are, oh, highness," Adam said stiffly. (I didn't see any big acting awards in his future.) "But there is a problem."

"A problem!?" Suzi cried dramatically. "What?"

"Snow White," Adam replied. "She's working hard to keep the planet clean. If she sees pollution coming from the castle, she might report you to the Environmental Protection Agency, or to the Planeteers."

"Curses!" Suzi snarled. (She was great!) "Then we must get rid of her! Woodsman! Where are you?"

At that moment, Vanessa was supposed to appear from the kitchen. But she didn't. "Where is that darn woodsman?" Suzi improvised.

"Vanessa," I called in a loud whisper.

"Jessi!" she called softly from the kitchen. "Come here."

"Cut!" Stacey called, turning off the camcorder. "What's wrong?"

Vanessa walked out dressed in green tights under gym shorts, a blousy shirt, and the felt hat we'd bought at Pembroke's. "This axe won't stay together," she explained. "See?" The head of the plastic axe came sliding off the plastic handle even as we spoke.

"Let me see that," I said, taking it from her. She was right. Nothing I did would keep the axe together. Then I got a bright idea and pulled out the elastic that was holding my hair back in a ponytail. With a few quick twists, I used it to keep the axe and the handle attached.

"Okay. Vanessa, you enter when I count to three," Stacey instructed her. The video then proceeded smoothly until Vanessa took Snow

White — played in the first scene by Carolyn Arnold — to the woods. (She and her twin sister, Marilyn, traded the black, plastic Snow White wig and the blue cloak back and forth in different scenes.)

"I'm sorry, but the queen has commanded me to get rid of you," said Vanessa to a cowering Snow White. She lifted her axe high into the air as if she were about to strike.

"Owww!" cried Buddy Barrett, who had been standing off to the side dressed in his Captain Planet costume. Vanessa's plastic axe blade had come loose and gone flying through the air, hitting Buddy on the head.

"Are you all right?" I asked, hurrying to him.

"I guess," he said sulkily as he rubbed his head.

The next scene was terrific. Instead of hurting Snow White, the Woodsman just pushed her into the swamp. (Vanessa thought of a good way to save the scene. "Darn!" she said. "My axe broke. Now I'll have to push you in the polluted swamp instead!") The swamp was a cardboard box covered with some green crêpe paper. We'd taped old cans and paper cups to it, to show that it was polluted. Snow White ducked behind the box. Then Haley Braddock, covered like a mummy in green crêpe paper, rose up out of the box where she'd been crouching. "I'll save you, Snow White," she said, pulling her to her feet. (Snow White was now Marilyn. Carolyn and Marilyn had switched places when they were behind the box.)

From there, Swamp Thing cast a magic spell that sent Snow White spinning into a rain forest where she met up with the Seven Zorbs. (We had our blow-up palm tree for the forest, and we taped the Disney animal characters on the walls. We also draped assorted rubber snakes, birds, and bugs around the room.) The zorbs came marching in, tooting on their plastic whistles. They wore their pointy ears and the paper cone hats we'd made. Marnie toddled in first as Dopey, then came Margo wearing her red nose and sneezing into a big white handkerchief. (She was Sneezy, of course.) Matt Braddock sneered as Grumpy, and Nicky Pike sucked his finger as Bashful. Laurel Kuhn played Doc and managed to look very scholarly. Norman Hill was Happy (the dwarf we'd had trouble remembering), and his sister Sarah was Sleepy. (The part *made* for Mallory!)

While the zorbs were singing, "Heigh Ho!" Suzi changed into her witch's costume. She presented the polluted apple to Snow White (who was now Carolyn, again). Snow White swooned to the floor. Her plastic wig tumbled off, but Stacey quickly panned to the zorbs

113

coming home from their diamond mines. (In this version, they were putting minerals and jewels back *into* the earth.)

"She shows all the signs of pollution poisoning!" cried Laurel as Doc. "We better call Captain Planet!" The zorbs put their plastic rings together and Buddy Barrett leaped into the room.

"I hear your call, Planeteer Zorbs!" he said. "How can I assist you?"

"You better do something about her!" said Sarah Hill pointing to the floor.

"I can see she's in bad shape," Buddy said. "Her hair has even fallen off." As he said that, Carolyn groped on the floor, her eyes still shut tight, and pulled her wig back on. "That's better," Buddy commented.

"Aren't you supposed to kiss her?" Laurel Kuhn asked.

Buddy glared at her. "No, Captain Planet never kisses anyone. I'll take her to my secret laboratory and give her the antidote to this poison. I want you zorbs to go get the wicked queen. Make sure she never pollutes again!"

A general cry of "Get the queen!" arose among the zorbs. In the next scene, Stacey had to dart around like crazy, trying to keep everyone in the picture as the zorbs ran after the queen, chasing her through the living room.

"Enough!" Suzi cried. "You zorbs win. I won't pollute anymore." She took her fake crown off her head and handed it to Laurel. "I'll give my crown and all my jewels to help clean up the planet." Everyone clapped, and then Snow White (now Marilyn) returned with Captain Planet.

"Snow White and I are going to stop pollution together from now on!" Buddy announced.

"Captain, honey!" Marilyn cried (which wasn't in the script) and planted a kiss on Buddy's cheek.

Buddy lost no time in wiping it off. "Yuck, Snow White! That's gross. It's cheek pollution!"

"Sorry." Marilyn giggled shyly.

Then, as we'd planned, the kids crowded together in a group. "Hi, Dawn!" they shouted. "We miss you!"

"Cut!" Stacey sang out happily as she took the camcorder from her eye. "Perfect!"

CHAPTER 13

Saturday

Dear Jessi,
   Hi! How are you? Things here are great. But I miss you and everyone a lot. I was missing baby-sitting, too. But now that's changed! I've joined the We ♡ Kids Club while I'm here. At least I won't be out of practice when I come back. Kids are pretty much the same on the West Coast as they are in the East. In fact, I worked on a project with my kids that I think you guys could try. It was so much fun!

I couldn't believe the rest of Dawn's letter! Guess what her project was? She made a video with the kids she baby-sits for!

Well, they say great minds think alike. Not only did our great minds think alike, but they thought alike on the same day. Dawn made her video while we were making *Snow White*.

Maybe I should back up and fill you in on a few things before I tell you about Dawn's video adventure. First of all, the We ♥ Kids Club is the California version of the BSC. When Dawn first joined the BSC here in Stoneybrook, she wrote her friend Sunny in California about the club and Sunny couldn't resist starting a club of her own.

Not long after that, the BSC took a trip to California and met the We ♥ Kids Club. Unfortunately, Kristy was appalled by how casually the club is run. They don't have officers, they are *not* strict about punctuality, and they don't even keep a notebook. They *do* have an appointment book, though, and they use Kid-Kits. And the We ♥ Kids Club has only three members — Sunny, Maggie, and Jill.

Well, they *had* only three members. Now they have four. *Our* Dawn.

Anyway, Dawn was sitting for three kids she'd known for a long time. The Clune kids — Sally (ten), Jenny (eight), and Jeannette (six). Dawn likes the kids a lot, but privately she calls them the Clones. That's because they look so much like one another. Each girl has short curly dark hair and big brown eyes.

When Dawn arrived at their house, the girls were draped across the lawn furniture on the back deck. "Ready to go into the pool?" she asked. The Clunes have a large above-ground pool in their yard.

"We've been in the pool everyday," Jenny complained.

Dawn tossed her beach towel onto a chair. "We don't have to go in, then," she said. "What else would you like to do?"

"You think of something," Jeannette told her.

Dawn tried to think of the things we had done while we were visiting. We'd had a blast — but we'd also had one advantage Dawn didn't have at that moment. We'd had transportation. Mr. Schafer's girlfriend, Carol, was incredibly generous with her time and chauffeured us wherever we wanted to go. (Dawn didn't always appreciate this because she didn't like Carol at the time, although now things are much better.)

But thinking about our visit is what gave Dawn her idea. "You know what?" she said to the kids. "My friends haven't been here in a long time. Maybe we could give them a 'video visit.' We could film the neighborhood, schools, and you and some of the other kids around here, and then send the video to my friends so they can see everything."

That's exactly what they did. Dawn returned to her house with the girls and found her dad's camcorder. Then she and the kids walked around the neighborhood. Their first stop was the home of two really wild kids named Erick and Ryan.

I'm sure this was for Kristy's benefit. She'd baby-sat for them when we visited. Naturally, Kristy, the conquering baby-sitter, had been able to manage them in the end, but they gave her a tough time in the beginning.

When Dawn and the Clune girls reached Erick and Ryan's house, they found the boys running around on their front lawn with the in-ground sprinklers on. The boys were wearing large, soaking-wet T-shirts, colorful knee-length beach jams, and matching over-sized sunglasses, and they were wielding Nerf Ball Master Blasters.

When they saw the girls approaching, Erick and Ryan assumed battle-ready positions, aiming their blasters at them. "Aaaaa-hhhhh!" Erick (who is eight) cried, doing his best imitation of Macaulay Culkin, from *Home Alone*. "We're under attack! Ready! Aim! Fire!"

The next thing Dawn knew she was ducking a volley of squishy orange balls. ("You'll see some wavery shots of sky and trees," Dawn said in her letter. "And you'll hear the girls squealing and me yelling, 'Cut it out! Put those guns away!' You *know* how I feel about guns!")

Their next stop was the house of a little girl named Stephie whom Mary Anne baby-sat for while we were on our vacation. When Dawn rang the bell, she came out with her new neighbor and friend, Margie. They were glad to demonstrate cartwheels which they'd just learned to do.

"Mary Anne will love to see Stephie looking so healthy and active," Dawn wrote. That's because Stephie has asthma. She even had an attack while Mary Anne was sitting for her. But Mary Anne learned that her attacks were brought on by emotional stress, not physical activity.

Mary Anne and Stephie had grown very close during the trip. They had a lot in common since they'd both lost their mothers at a young age and both had over-protective fathers. (Mr. Spier had been way too protective of Mary Anne until he met Dawn's mother. Then he loosened up a lot.)

After Dawn and the Clones (I mean the Clunes) said good-bye to Stephie and Margie they went to the school Dawn is attending, and then to the elementary school the Clunes attend.

Their final stop was back at Dawn's house for a tour of her home. Jeff, Dawn's younger brother, was there playing checkers with Carol in the kitchen. Jeff and Carol sang the chorus of "Uncle John's Band," which is a song by the Grateful Dead. (Jeff considers himself a major "Deadhead.") Mr. Schafer waved to the camera.

"This will be a real blast from the past for you guys," Dawn concluded at the end of her letter. "I wanted to keep it a secret and surprise you, but I just couldn't resist telling you it was coming. When I called Mary Anne yesterday she said there was a surprise coming my way, too. I can't wait. Mary Anne is better at keeping a secret than I am. She wouldn't tell what it was. I guess I'll just have to be surprised."

Boy, would she *ever* be surprised. As far as I could tell from the date of her letter, at this very moment our two videos were probably crossing midair as they were flown from one coast to the other!

CHAPTER 14

At our next BSC meeting on Monday, I sat and waited anxiously, keeping my fingers crossed that Wendy would show up at five-thirty. I really didn't want another tense scene between Kristy and Wendy. Since I'd brought Wendy into the club I couldn't help but feel responsible for her.

"You're worried about Wendy, aren't you?" observed Mallory from her spot at my right side.

"How can you tell?" I asked.

"You haven't taken your eye off the door since you got here."

I smiled and turned toward her. "How are you feeling?"

"A little better," she said. "The resting helps. I just hope I'll feel completely normal soon. Feeling crummy all the time is sort of depressing."

"I can imagine."

122

At 5:29 I heaved a sigh of relief as Wendy came through Claudia's bedroom door. My smile faded, though, when I saw the look on her face. Her mouth was set in a thin line and her big brown eyes were narrowed and angry. "What's wrong?" I whispered as she sat down beside me on the floor.

She shrugged. "I was having a good time hanging out with some friends of mine. We were having a big Super Mario Brothers tournament. I was winning and then I just had to drop it to come here."

"It's important that you're here," I said. To me, a club meeting seemed much more important than winning a video game. But then, I've never been a video game lover.

Wendy nodded but she looked unconvinced.

At the stroke of five-thirty, as usual, Kristy called the meeting to order. "I have some business I'd like to get out of the way," she said immediately. "First, I spoke to Shannon today and she's going to be here in a little while but she'll be late. Second, Wendy, I've heard that you were pretty late for the job at the Pikes' the other day."

Wendy looked at me sharply, her eyes full of accusation.

"I told her," Mary Anne spoke up. "I didn't do it to be mean, Wendy. But Kristy is the club president. It's the kind of thing I think she should know about."

"I was fifteen, maybe twenty minutes late," Wendy said defensively. "Jessi was already there. I don't see the big deal."

"The big deal is that when parents call here they know they can count on us in every way," Kristy countered snippily. "That means they can be confident that they can get out the door when they need to. This business works because we run it in a professional manner."

Wendy opened her mouth to speak. Then she closed it and crossed her arms. She seemed undecided about something, but finally she spoke. "I don't think this is working out for me."

"Why is that?" Stacey spoke levelly. I think she was hoping to diffuse the tension between Kristy and Wendy.

"Too many rules," Wendy said. "I like to do things my own way. My own way works for me."

"Is that all?" Claudia asked.

"No," Wendy admitted. "There are other reasons. I don't particularly like the idea that I have to turn all my jobs over to you guys. And I don't really want to have to be here three times a week, either. It takes up too much time."

"You knew the rules when you joined," Kristy said.

"No, actually, I didn't," Wendy replied. "The meeting I attended was so frantic that no one ever really explained them to me. All I knew was that Jessi's crazy about the club. So I figured it must be great. And, it is great — for you. But not for me."

"Maybe this has just been an adjustment period," Mary Anne said.

Wendy got to her feet and shook her head. "No, I don't think so. I have parents. I have teachers. I don't need a club telling me what to do, too." She aimed her next remark at Kristy. "That's just one too many people bossing me around. Sorry it didn't work out. 'Bye."

Without even looking at me, Wendy left the room.

"Good-bye." Kristy spat out the words. "No offense, Jessi. But I can't believe you and she are friends."

"Wendy is pretty independent," I said.

"Maybe you've finally met your match, Kristy." Stacey laughed.

Kristy glared at her. "Wendy? Not likely. I don't think there's much value in being completely undisciplined and unable to follow a few simple rules."

I agreed with Kristy, but I also knew what Stacey was getting at. As much as they disliked each other, Kristy and Wendy were both headstrong and determined to do things their own way. They had a lot in common. The difference was that Kristy was a leader, and Wendy was a loner.

"It looks like we're back where we started from," said Mary Anne.

"I'm sorry she didn't work out," I told my friends. "I feel like I've let you guys down, but I honestly did think she'd be a good club member."

"It's okay," Kristy said. "You didn't know. You tried. I'm relieved that she quit. If she kept being late like that we'd have had to ask her to leave and that would have been pretty unpleasant."

"I had an actual nightmare over that," Mary Anne said. "I had it last night. I dreamed we all had to stand in a circle and tell Wendy why she had to leave. In the dream, I couldn't do anything but cry because I felt so bad for her."

"My mother says the thing she hates most about her job is when she has to fire someone," Kristy said. "But sometimes she just *has* to."

At that moment, Shannon came in. "Hi, everybody," she said brightly as she pulled off her jacket. "Sorry I'm late, but I had the very last meeting of the Honor Society dinner committee. The dinner is tomorrow. Thank goodness. It was *so* much work."

"That's good news," said Claudia. "Because we just lost our new member."

Shannon pulled off her red felt hat and shook out her hair. "From what Kristy told me she wasn't working out too well, anyway. When is Dawn coming back?"

"Not for months," Claudia grumbled. "That is *if* she comes back."

"She'll be back," Mary Anne said.

"Well, listen, I had an idea," said Shannon as she perched on the end of Claudia's bed. "Since you guys have been calling me a zillion times every meeting anyway, why don't I just come to the meetings and be the alternate officer until Dawn returns? Then when she gets back, if you don't need me, I'll go back to my old position as associate member."

"That's perfect!" Kristy cried.

"You don't think you'll mind stepping back down?" Mary Anne asked cautiously. "I mean, you know, it might be hard."

"It'll be spring by then," Shannon pointed out. "I'll be happy to have the time off to do outdoor stuff. Plus, I'm always really busy with school stuff. And my parents are talking about going to the shore, and I'll probably go to camp again this summer, so I might not even be around then, anyway."

"You can't go!" Kristy said urgently. "What will we do if we need you?"

"Relax," Stacey laughed. "We just solved one problem. Right now the summer seems very far away. Let's worry about that then."

"All right," Kristy said with a smile.

The phone rang then and we didn't have a moment to do anything but see who could take each job that was called in. Shannon was a lifesaver. She took a lot of jobs. We finally seemed to be back on track. Once again we were the smooth-running BSC I was used to.

Not until I was walking toward my house, the fleecy collar of my denim jacket turned up against the wind and my hands jammed in my pockets, did I think about Wendy again. I had liked her so much when I met her.

Did I still like her?

She *had* let me down. And she had been sharp with Kristy, who was a good friend of mine. And now I knew she was unreliable — at least as far as being on time.

But I couldn't stop thinking about how much fun I had with her. She was always full of energy and in a good mood.

Wendy hadn't done anything terrible to me.

And Kristy had treated her in her usual forth-right Kristy way. I'm so used to Kristy now that I forget she takes a little getting used to at first. Having a friend who wasn't punctual wasn't the end of the world, either. It might be annoying from time to time, but I could live with that.

As I climbed the front steps to my house, another thought hit me. Even if I was willing to be friends with Wendy — was she still willing to be friends with me?

That's when I knew I really did want to continue my friendship with Wendy. The thought of her not wanting to be my friend anymore made me feel terrible.

"Hi," Mama greeted me when I entered the living room. She was on the floor building a tower of blocks with Squirt. "You look pretty serious," she observed.

"It's Wendy," I said. "Remember when I told you she was going to join the club?"

Mama nodded.

"Well, she quit today and now I'm afraid she won't want to be friends with me any-more."

"Did she say that?" Mama asked.

"No. We didn't get a chance to talk."

"Then maybe you should call her," she suggested as Squirt added the block that sent the tower crashing to the floor.

While I was hanging up my jacket, I decided she was right. There was no sense wondering about it all evening until I saw Wendy at school the next day. I went into the kitchen and punched in Wendy's number. "Hi, it's me, Jessi," I said when she picked up the phone.

"Hi," she said. A terrible, awkward silence hung between us.

"Just get it over with," she said finally.

"What?" I asked.

"You're mad at me, right? So just say what you have to say!"

"I'm not mad at you," I told her. "I thought you were mad at me."

"Why should I be mad at you?" she asked.

"I don't know," I admitted. "I just figured you hated me and everything connected with the Baby-sitters Club."

"No way!" Wendy exclaimed. "It's just not for me, but I don't hate it. I don't even hate Kristy, even though she's not my favorite person on earth. The BSC works for you guys, but I couldn't fit into it. That's all."

"I know where you would have fit in perfectly," I told her, the idea suddenly occurring to me. "If you lived near Dawn in California, you'd do well in the baby-sitting club there. The We ♥ Kids Club is much less formal, much looser. Kristy was totally appalled by it."

That made Wendy laugh. "I'll bet she was. I probably would have loved it, then. Too bad I don't live in California."

"No, I'm *glad* you don't," I said seriously. "One good friend in California is plenty."

CHAPTER 15

"Look out! Look out!" Mallory screamed as she careened toward Kristy and me, her arms flapping like a crazy bird trying to get off the ground. The roller skates on her feet were spinning at full speed.

"Whoa!" Kristy laughed, catching hold of Mal and steadying her.

Mallory panted as she worked to keep her balance. It was Saturday and the members of the BSC had the morning off. By some miracle, not one of us had a job until four that afternoon. So we had decided to go roller skating in the schoolyard.

"I've never been good at this," Mallory complained good-naturedly. She pointed to the rollerblade in-line skates on Kristy's feet. "And those would knock me cold in about three seconds."

"Nah, you just have to get used to them," Kristy said, tightening her helmet. She pushed off and skated a fast circle around the empty cement basketball court.

Stacey and Claudia were also on roller-blades, but they were busy clinging to the chain-link fence around the court. Every so often, they would venture out on their skates. Even if they weren't the greatest skaters, they looked terrific. Claudia wore hot pink stirrup pants and a fuzzy pink sweater that made a nice contrast with her neon green pads and helmet. Stacey looked cool as ever in jeans and a short brown leather jacket. Her helmet was black with silver streaks.

Shannon, Mal, and I were using regular old roller skates, but we were having fun. At least Shannon and I were. Mal was flopping a lot, but she was moving and laughing. Compared to the droopy Mal of a week ago, this was a good sign.

"Is it lunchtime yet?" Mal asked hopefully.

Mary Anne looked at her watch and nodded. "Pizza time."

"All right!" Mallory cried.

We took off our skates, left the schoolyard, and began the walk downtown. At Pizza Express we ordered a large pie with pepperoni. Everyone agreed that the one and only good thing about Dawn's being gone was that we didn't have to order half the pie plain or with veggies, since Dawn doesn't eat red meat.

"I wonder if Dawn got our video yet," I said, wiping tomato sauce off my chin.

"We'll probably hear from her when she gets it," said Kristy. "After all, we haven't received hers, either."

In no time flat, the pizza was devoured. I noticed that Mal hadn't finished her slice. "Are you all right?" I asked her quietly.

"Yeah, but I started to feel a little strange. Just dizzy," she said. "I'm okay, though."

"You probably shouldn't have come out skating," I said. "Rest when you get home."

Mallory rolled her eyes. "I'm rested out. I couldn't care less if I never rest again. But I guess you're right. Skating was probably pushing things a bit."

"How's Margo doing?" I asked her.

"She's not in jail, if that's what you mean," said Mal.

"I didn't mean that!"

"I was just kidding," Mallory said. "She's fine. You won't believe this, but she thanked me for insisting she tell Mom. She said to thank you, too. She knew what she was doing was wrong. It was giving her guilt stomach-aches. She hasn't had a single one since she gave the stuff back."

"Great," I said.

When we left Pizza Express we walked together back to Claudia's house. That's where we'd originally met that morning and each of us had left a jacket or a bag or something there that we now had to retrieve. As soon as we walked in the door, Claudia spotted a small package wrapped in brown paper sitting on the front hall table. It was addressed to the BSC. "It's from Dawn," said Claudia, reading the return address.

In a flash she tore open the paper. It was the video!

"Play it!" Kristy said eagerly.

We hurried into the Kishis' living room and Claud popped the video into the VCR. Instantly Dawn's smiling face came on the screen. "Hi, guys!" she said brightly. "Since you can't be in California, I'm bringing it to you. My guests today are Sally, Jenny, and Jeannette Clune. Our special guests will be . . . brace yourself, Kristy." Here Dawn crossed her eyes. "Total terrors Erick and Ryan, plus the very sweet Stephanie Robertson. We're not sure if they're home yet, but we're going to try to find them."

Everyone laughed at Erick and Ryan. "Poor Dawn," Shannon said as the volley of orange Nerf Balls flew toward the camera lens.

"She looks great," said Mary Anne. "I heard a touch of anxiety in her voice. I think she was worried that Dawn was having *too* good a time.

When the video ended, Claudia let her chin drop into her hands. "Boy, this makes me miss Dawn even more."

We all nodded sadly. "It shows she's thinking of us, though," I said, mostly for Mary Anne's sake. The growing tinge of pink at the tip of her nose told me she was on the verge of tears.

Kristy noticed it, too. "I say we use some club money to call Dawn," she suggested.

"Sure, we have enough money, almost," Stacey agreed. "We will by next week, anyway."

The phone upstairs in Claudia's room began to ring just then. "Who could that be?" Claudia wondered. She jumped to her feet and ran upstairs.

"Dawn!" she screamed excitedly. We could hear her all the way down in the living room. Instantly we thundered up the stairs to join in on the phone call.

"We just finished watching your video," Claudia was telling her as we ran into the room. "It was great!" Claudia cupped her hand around the phone and turned to us. "It's Dawn."

"Duh," said Kristy.

"She got our video today," Claudia added. "She thinks it's hysterical."

My friends and I started yelling, "Let me

talk to her! I want to talk to her!" all at the same time.

Finally my turn came. "Hi, Dawn!"

"Jessi, I couldn't stop laughing," she told me. "When Snow White's wig popped off, I thought I would die. I laughed so hard I cried. And I can't believe we both had the same idea at the same time."

"I know, it's pretty amazing," I agreed. "Actually, Buddy and Suzi Barrett first had the idea."

"Oh, they were a riot. Buddy as Captain Planet was too funny. And Suzi was really good. She's growing up. I miss them."

"They miss you, too," I told her. "That's why they wanted to make the video. So you wouldn't forget them."

"I couldn't forget them."

"Your video was great, too," I said.

"Thanks, but it wasn't nearly as creative as yours. My next one will be better."

"Next one?"

"Sure. This is a great way to stay in touch."

Unexpectedly, I felt a lump form in my throat. "You *are* coming back, aren't you?" I managed to say.

"Jessi, of course I am," she replied. "Don't worry."

"Okay."

Stacey was dying to get on the phone, so I

said good-bye to Dawn and handed Stacey the receiver. Stacey only got to talk for three minutes before Claudia, Kristy, Mary Anne, and Shannon started hovering near her trying to hear, giggling and shouting things to Dawn all the while.

"Do you really think she'll come back?" I asked Mallory who was sitting on the bed.

"I think so," said Mal. "How could she leave friends like this behind?"

As I looked at my happy, laughing friends, I knew what Mal meant. Dawn would never find better friends than these.

And neither would I.

The Baby-sitters Club was (almost) back to normal.

About the Author

ANN M. MARTIN did *a lot* of baby-sitting when she was growing up in Princeton, New Jersey. She is a former editor of books for children, and was graduated from Smith College.

Ms. Martin lives in New York City with her cats, Mouse and Rosie. She likes ice cream and *I Love Lucy*; and she hates to cook.

Ann Martin's Apple Paperbacks include *Yours Turly, Shirley*; *Ten Kids, No Pets*; *With You and Without You*; *Bummer Summer*; and all the other books in the Baby-sitters Club series.

Look for BSC #69

GET WELL SOON, MALLORY!

I had planned to go trick-or-treating with my best friend Jessica Ramsey and her brother and sister, but by the time I'd passed out bags and talked Claire into wearing a coat over her tutu, I was too exhausted to walk anywhere. So I gave her a call.

"Jessi, I think I'm going to stay home tonight. I'm really tired."

"What'd you do," she asked, "stay up late last night?"

"No, I fell asleep after dinner and didn't wake up till eleven this morning."

"That's strange," Jessi said. "Are you sick?"

I felt my forehead. "I don't have a fever, or a cold, or anything like that," I explained. "I just feel worn out."

"Well, you better not come with us, then

Squirt and Becca are so excited, they'll probably run the entire night."

(Squirt is Jessi's nickname for her baby brother, who's only one-and-a-half. Becca's her eight-and-a-half year old sister and looks like a younger version of Jessi.

"Sorry to back out on you," I mumbled.

"That's okay," Jessi said. "I understand."

"Oh, one more thing," I said before we hung up. "My family's going to New York for Thanksgiving."

"Mal, that's fantastic!" Jessi squealed.

I silently wished I was as enthusiastic about it as Jessi. I had a really uneasy feeling inside. What if I was still sick in three weeks? It'd be awful to go all that way and feel this lousy. I'd ruin the whole vacation.

We said good-bye and I sat at my desk, trying to catch up on my work. I'd missed a lot of school as I caught cold after cold and the homework had really started to pile up. The more I stared at my math, the more blurry-eyed I felt. Finally I shut my math book and lay my head on top of the desk. I decided to take a little nap before all of the trick-or-treaters started ringing our bell.

Read all the books
in the Baby-sitters Club series
by Ann M. Martin

#10 *Sea City, Here We Come!*
The Baby-sitters head back to the Jersey shore for
some fun in the sun!

Mysteries:

1 *Stacey and the Missing Ring*
Stacey's being accused of taking a valuable ring.
Can the Baby-sitters help clear her name?

2 *Beware, Dawn!*
Someone is playing pranks on Dawn when she's
baby-sitting — and they're *not* funny.

3 *Mallory and the Ghost Cat*
It looks and sounds like a cat — but is it real?

4 *Kristy and the Missing Child*
Kristy organizes a search party to help the police
find a missing child.

5 *Mary Anne and the Secret in the Attic*
Mary Anne discovers a secret about her past and
now she's afraid of the future!

6 *The Mystery at Claudia's House*
Claudia's room has been ransacked! Can the Baby-
sitters track down whodunnit?

7 *Dawn and the Disappearing Dogs*
Someone's been stealing dogs all over Stoneybrook!

8 *Jessi and the Jewel Thieves*
Jessi and her friend Quint are busy tailing two
jewel thieves all over the Big Apple!

9 *Kristy and the Haunted Mansion*
Kristy and the Krashers are spending the night in
a spooky old house!

THE BABY-SITTERS CLUB®

by Ann M. Martin

More titles... ▶

The Baby-sitters Club titles continued...

Available wherever you buy books...or use this order form.

Scholastic Inc., P.O. Box 7502, 2931 E. McCarty Street, Jefferson City, MO 65102

Please send me the books I have checked above. I am enclosing $———
(please add $2.00 to cover shipping and handling). Send check or money order - no cash or C.O.D.s please.

Name ——————————————————————————————

Address ——————————————————————————————

City———————————————— State/Zip ————————————

Please allow four to six weeks for delivery. Offer good in the U.S. only. Sorry, mail orders are not available to residents of Canada. Prices subject to change.

How would YOU like to visit Universal Studios in Orlando, Florida?

Check out the sights!

Experience the rides!

Tour the Studios!

Enter  **THE BABY-SITTERS CLUB®**

Summer Super Special Giveaway for your chance to win!

We'll send one grand prize winner and a parent or guardian on an all expense paid trip to Universal Studios in Orlando, Florida for 3 days and 2 nights!

25 second prize winners receive a Baby-sitters Club Fun Pack filled with a Baby-sitters Club T-Shirt, "Songs For My Best Friends" cassette, Baby-sitters Club stationery and more!

All you have to do is fill out the coupon below or write the information
on a 3" x 5" piece of paper and mail to:
**THE BABY-SITTERS CLUB SUMMER SUPER SPECIAL GIVEAWAY P.O. Box 7500,
Jefferson City, MO 65102. Return by November 30 1993.**

- -

THE SUMMER SUPER SPECIAL GIVEAWAY

Name_____ Birthdate _____

Address _____

City_____ State/Zip _____

Rules: Entries must be postmarked by November 30, 1993. Winners will be picked at random and notified by mail. No purchase necessary. Valid only in the U.S. Void where prohibited. Taxes on prizes are the responsibility of the winners and their immediate families. Employees of Scholastic Inc; its agencies, affiliates, subsidiaries, and their immediate families not eligible. For a complete list of winners, send a self-addresses stamped envelope to:The Baby-sitters Club Summer Super Special Giveaway, Winners List, after November 30 at the address provided above.

BSC693

NOW PLAYING!

Home Video Collection

*Look for these
all new episodes!*

•

**Claudia and the Mystery
of the Secret Passage**

Dawn Saves the Trees

The Baby-sitters and the Boy Sitters

**Jessi and the Mystery
of the Stolen Secrets**

Stacey Takes a Stand

The Baby-sitters Remember

•

*Available wherever fun
videos are sold*